A HORSE TO LOVE

NANCY SPRINGER

A Horse to Love

————— HARPER & ROW, PUBLISHERS —————
Grand Rapids, Philadelphia, St. Louis, San Francisco, London,
Singapore, Sydney, Tokyo, Toronto
————— NEW YORK —————

Library of Congress Cataloging-in-Publication Data
Springer, Nancy.
  A horse to love.

  Summary: With some help, a girl learns that
owning and caring for her dream horse is both
frustrating and rewarding.
  1. Horses—Juvenile fiction. [1.Horses—Fiction.
I. Title.
PZ10.3.S683Ho 1987   [Fic]   86-45487
ISBN 0-06-025824-1
ISBN 0-06-025825-X (lib. bdg.)

3 4 5 6 7 8 9 10

To Jean Wertz,
who should have been an editor

A HORSE TO LOVE

Chapter One

"Oh, wow, she's pretty!" Erin whispered.

"Don't get your hopes up," Aunt Lexie warned her.

Erin knew better than to get her hopes up. The last horse had been a nag with a Roman nose and a goose rump and the name, really and truly, of Pig-poop. All of which would have been okay if it had been willing, eager to please, but it was not.

"Pretty is as pretty does," Aunt Lexie added darkly.

The horse before that had been a pretty chestnut gelding with a cream-colored mane and tail, but he had been too coltish, too much of a handful for a young rider. The horse before that had been a nice black mare that Erin's father might have bought except that the owner, while showing off her beautiful canter, had decided not to sell her after all. The horse before that had been a dark bay that was nippy and spoiled.

This one, Erin thought, was prettier than any of them.

"She looks kind of fat," said Erin's father doubtfully. "Is she—uh—pregnant?"

"Hay belly," said Aunt Lexie. "Needs to be worked."

The mare had been out to pasture, and the man was leading her toward them. "Grade mare, gray, 10 yrs," the ad in the paper had read, meaning just a regular horse, not registered anything. Erin's father had been singing "The Old Gray Mare" in the car all the way over. Slumped in the backseat of Aunt Lexie's Blazer, Erin had come to expect a sway-backed nag built like a plow horse. But the little mare walking toward them was more white than gray, with a pretty white face, a dark nose, and big dark eyes that made Erin think of a deer's eyes. Her small white ears were pricked forward, her forelock lying gray between them, and her head nodded at every step. The man led her up to them and turned her sideways so that they could look at her.

Aunt Lexie chewed at the stem of her pipe, her eyes hard and narrow as she studied the mare. She was not Erin's aunt, not really, but the woman who lived half a mile down the road and raised Morgan horses. The other kids in the neighborhood knew her as Mrs. Bromer (or Old Baggy Bromer, among themselves), and knew that she didn't let anyone touch her horses. When she had said to Erin, "You may call me Aunt Lexie," Erin had understood at once that the "Aunt" was required. Erin called all her real aunts and uncles by their first names, but Alexandra Elizabeth Bromer was older than them and not to be messed with.

Erin tore her gaze away from the mare's pretty head—Aunt Lexie said that only a novice looked first at a horse's head. No feet, no horse. She studied the mare's hooves and legs. They were charcoal gray, like her nose, and Erin thought they looked okay, straight and solid. She would not find out what Aunt Lexie thought until afterward, on the way home. It would be a bad idea to say anything about good legs in front of the owner. He might raise the price. Erin wanted to go over and pat the mare, but she was not supposed to seem too eager.

"Just lift her feet for us," Aunt Lexie ordered the man in a bored tone.

One of her many rules: Never do anything with a horse that the owner won't do first. If the mare tried to kick the man, that would be the end of it. He tied her to a fence post by the halter rope and lifted one forefoot—no problem. He lifted the feet one by one, and the mare did not seem to mind at all.

"All right, Erin, you do it," said Aunt Lexie.

At last, a chance to get her hands on her. . . .

With the adult eyes watching, Erin remembered to hold back her smile, to walk, not run, over to the mare. But she took her time once she got there, patting the horse on the neck, looking into her big, dark eye, speaking softly.

"Hi, girl. How are you today?"

The mare looked back without blinking. Not a kind eye, Erin decided, but at least a soft eye. The large, barlike pupil glinted blue in the sunlight. Erin turned and bent, ran her hand down the foreleg and tugged at the front foot. After a moment it came up. She moved to the hind foot, listening for the tail swish that might come before a kick, feeling for tightness in the horse's muscles. All was well, and the mare gave the foot.

"Should I saddle her up?" the man asked.

"Might as well," said Aunt Lexie, taking her pipe out of her mouth to yawn.

They followed the man into the remodeled cow barn that served as a stable. Erin and her father knew the routine by now.

"She bite?" Mr. Calahan asked.

"Nope."

"Kick?"

"Nope."

"Spook?"

"Nope. Well, I mean, there ain't none of them won't spook at something. But I ain't knowed her to spook hard. We ride her along the road, and she don't mind cars or trucks or dogs."

"Motorcycles?" asked Aunt Lexie with a hard look. "Gunshots?"

"No problem."

"Why are you selling her?" asked Mr. Calahan, and the man shrugged.

"Too many horses."

That certainly could be true. Nearly every stall in the barn had a horse in it, or a pony, all shapes and sizes and colors of horses and ponies, and there were more in the pasture. Erin, who was used to the bay and chestnut Morgans at Aunt Lexie's, looked at roans, sorrels, Appaloosas with widened eyes.

"I bought her for my granddaughter, for pole bending," the man offered, "but she ain't fast enough for that. So now I bought that one there." He pointed toward a handsome pinto that was kicking at its stall. When Erin glanced toward it, the pinto pinned back its ears and bared its teeth at her.

She quickly turned back to the "old gray mare" and watched, along with Aunt Lexie, as the owner put on a western saddle and a bridle with a western bit and clip-on reins. The mare stood quietly as he tightened the cinch, and she took the bit willingly.

"Want to try her, missie?" the man offered when he had led the horse out. "Her name's Bianca."

"*You* ride her out," said Aunt Lexie before Erin could reply.

The man heaved himself into the saddle—the mare moved forward a few steps, Erin noticed, but no wonder, as he had jabbed his toe into her ribs. He took her out along the road at a rapid walk, brought her back at the trot. Bianca nodded her head at the walk, stuck her nose out high at the trot. The owner stopped her in front of Erin.

"Want to try her now?"

Erin glanced at Aunt Lexie, who nodded. "But I've never ridden western," Erin said.

"Just sit to the trot."

"Nothing to it," the man told her. He boosted her up and handed her the reins.

"Wait," Aunt Lexie said. "Those stirrups are way too long." But the horse had already started off. Erin sat watching the eager white ears in front of her. She felt secure in the big saddle, even though her feet were swinging. She had ridden without stirrups before. Reins in both hands, as she had been taught, she let the horse walk out to the end of the driveway, nudged with her right leg and tightened her fingers on the right rein to turn her onto the shoulder of the road. . . .

The mare tossed her head up and fought the bit, dancing sideways.

"Neck rein her!" the owner hollered. "She rides western!"

"Hold both reins in one hand!" Aunt Lexie shouted.

Erin had already let go with her left hand. But her right hand missed catching hold of the other rein, somehow, in her hurry, and these reins did not loop over the horse's neck like the English ones she was used to. Each was separate from the other. And the one she had dropped slithered down and slapped the dirt beneath the mare's head.

"Whoa!" Erin exclaimed, tugging harder on her one remaining rein. The mare shook her head and fussed, prancing nearly onto the road.

"Oh, no," Erin moaned. "Bianca, please whoa. There's traffic coming." Scared, she grabbed at the saddle horn with her free hand.

Bianca stepped on the trailing rein and flung her head up sharply. Erin could see the flash of white in a frightened eye. Helpless, she sat clutching the saddle horn, not knowing what to expect next. She did not dare to pull on her rein again. Suppose Bianca fought her way even farther onto the road? But the mare did not move. Head up, ears tilted at a troubled sideward angle, she stood stone-still as a pickup truck and three motorcycles whizzed past her nose with a bone-jarring racket. By the time they were gone, Aunt Lexie had reached Erin's side, and so had her father and the horse owner.

"Back, girl," he said to Bianca, taking her by the cheek strap of the bridle. The mare stepped back, and the man picked up the trailing rein.

"She has good sense," Aunt Lexie remarked, patting Bianca on the neck to calm her.

"Here you go, missie. I'll tie 'em together for you." The man knotted the reins into one and handed them to Erin. "Just push 'em against her neck, whichever way you want to go."

Erin sat choking back an urge to cry. She felt stupid and embarrassed; she was frightened, and she knew she wanted this pretty little mare. If she wanted her, she had to ride her. Good sense, Aunt Lexie had said, right in front of the owner. . . .

Taking a deep breath, Erin squeezed with her legs, lifted the reins with one hand and clicked her tongue. Neck reining, she turned Bianca so that they were riding alongside the road. The mare walked willingly, and within a few strides her ears pricked forward again and Erin felt her relax. They reached an open space. Erin did several small circles, both directions, trying out the neck reining, then took the horse back. She did not feel like trotting. Cars went past—the mare did not mind them. Erin brought Bianca to a stop in front of the others.

"See if she'll back up," Aunt Lexie said.

"Back," Erin ordered, tugging on the reins. The mare tossed her head and fussed, starting to dance again. Erin's heart sank.

"Okay," said Aunt Lexie. "Just walk her back to the barn."

The old woman did not sound too disgusted. Perhaps there was a chance of buying the mare after all.

Erin dismounted and stood, trying not to fidget, as she listened to the adults talking. She could not tell anything from their polite chatter. At last, by some unspoken agreement, it was time to go. She slid into the backseat of the Blazer and waited. It did not occur to her to say that she liked and wanted the horse. Erin was not much in the habit of speaking up. Crumpled in her corner, she waited for the adults to hand down judgment.

"That's a nice little mare," Aunt Lexie said.

Erin's father looked at the older woman in surprise. He knew very little about horses, although he was starting to learn for Erin's sake.

"Nice size for Erin, fifteen hands," Mrs. Bromer continued. "Old enough to have sense, willing enough, nice and calm."

"She didn't look calm to me!" Mr. Calahan protested.

"Only because of that ridiculous bit the man has on her." Aunt Lexie's voice rose. "Eight-inch shanks! And a port the size of Gibraltar. Every time you touch her mouth with that thing, she goes crazy. If she wasn't such a quiet horse, she would have thrown him before now."

"Oh, no," said Erin, prodded out of silence by her own shame. "And I tugged on her. I'm so stupid—"

"Stop that," Aunt Lexie snapped. "You did fine. I should have told you to neck rein, is all. Horse doesn't have to come on the bit that way. English, you touched her mouth and she went bananas."

"I thought we wanted an English riding horse." Mr. Calahan sounded exasperated, perhaps by all the jargon he did not yet understand.

"She'll be able to rein her English on a lighter bit. Erin has nice light hands, and there's a good soft mouth on that mare."

Yowsers! thought Erin, I might really get this one. My own horse! Oh, wow! A real horse. Bianca—I can give her a better name—omigoodness, come on, Aunt Lexie!

"But the horse misbehaved!" Mr. Calahan was wearing a stubborn expression. "It walked off with her!"

"Just so it didn't run off with her," said Aunt Lexie severely. "That man has let his horses forget their manners. Once she's reminded, she'll remember." Alexandra Elizabeth Bromer stared hard at Mr. Calahan. "You're never going to find the exact perfect horse. Not at the price."

That last was a strong point. Breathless, Erin watched her father's stubborn expression fade into one of doubt.

"I don't know. . . . She sure didn't look like much to me."

Aunt Lexie snorted. "She's been out to grass, that's why! Horses get fat and flabby just like people. That's why she has that big belly and no muscle in her quarters. But she has nice straight legs, hard hooves, nice slope to her shoulder, neck set on well, nice high withers to hold a saddle. Nice level back." She stared again. "If she were in condition she'd cost you three times as much."

"I just don't know," said Mr. Calahan.

Even though she was not used to speaking up,

Erin was so anxious that she could keep silent no longer. "Dad," she begged, *"please."*

Her father turned and looked at her, surprised, as if he had forgotten she was there.

"I like her," Erin added in a small voice. "She's nice." She did not say "pretty" because she knew the adults would laugh at her, but Mr. Calahan laughed anyway.

"That goes without saying, Squirt. Show me a horse you don't like!"

She hated it when he laughed and called her Squirt, but she didn't tell him so. She never had. Least of all this time, when she felt so close to having a horse of her own, if only he would buy it for her.

He turned solemn, looking at her. "I don't know, Erin. It's so iffy. The horse is supposed to get back in condition, remember her manners, learn to rein English—"

"It's always iffy with horses," said Aunt Lexie in a matter-of-fact tone.

"Oh. Well . . . " Mr. Calahan looked hard at Erin. "You remember our agreement, Squirt?"

She nodded, trying not to bounce with impatience. The agreement had been worked out during weeks of bargaining with her parents. If she wanted them to buy her a horse, she was to keep her grades up. She was to have no other gifts until Christmas. She was to mend her clothes and spend no money unwisely. She was to clean her room, change her bed, and help with the household chores.

Her father turned back to Aunt Lexie.

"So what do we do? Call the man and tell him we'll take her?"

Yaaah-hooo! Erin shrieked mentally.

"Have her vetted first."

Oh no. If the vet finds anything wrong, I am going to die, Erin thought.

"Horse has more sense than most people I know," Aunt Lexie muttered. "More sense than— Do you realize that most horses would have gone totally out of control when they stepped on that rein?"

"So why does the man want to sell her?" Mr. Calahan retorted.

"He's a fool. Likes them young and flashy and hard to handle. Stupid." She curled her wrinkled brown fingers around the steering wheel of her Blazer in a forceful way as she drove them home.

Oh, wow, maybe really my own horse, finally! Go riding all spring, all summer, down the pasture lane and along the woods behind the development. . . .

Terrace Heights, the builders called it. Erin's family lived there to be near the small Pennsylvania city where her father had his photography studio. Erin did not very much like their house, which was called a "rancher," and which was not at all like any ranch house she had ever imagined. It didn't have much yard, either. She had been disappointed when her family had moved in two years before. But there was still country behind the houses and the industrial park, and there was a marvelous place just a short bike ride down the road: Willow Hill Farm, Mrs. Bromer's breeding stable, forty acres of green amid the built-up surroundings. Ever since she could remember, Erin had wanted a horse, and though she knew from the other kids that she would be yelled at and chased away if she tried to touch Mrs. Bromer's horses, still . . . It did no harm to stand by the fence for hours, just watching. . . .

Aunt Lexie pulled into the driveway. A welcoming whinny sounded from the stable. Erin and her father got out and headed for their own car to go home for Sunday supper.

"Well," said Mr. Calahan to Aunt Lexie, "thanks."

"I'll call the vet tomorrow," said Alexandra Bromer. "Probably take him a week or two to get out there."

A week or two!

"You call that man and tell him we're interested and make sure he gives us first refusal," she ordered.

"Okay," said Mr. Calahan meekly. He got into his Toyota with the thankful look of someone making an escape. "Be glad that woman's your friend, Squirt," he remarked to Erin as they drove home.

Supper was ham sandwiches. Erin's mother was working. She was assistant manager at the hospital cafeteria and worked alternate Sundays. Erin's older brother, Mike, was home. Erin knew better than to say much about her horse to him. He would be sure to make fun of her somehow. She kept quiet, but she was so excited that she could hardly eat.

"Are you going to call the man now, Dad?" she asked as soon as they were finished.

"Huh?" Mr. Calahan stared a moment as if he had forgotten about it, then looked at his watch. "I'll call him tomorrow evening."

Tomorrow evening! "But, Dad—"

"He won't sell the horse before then, Squirt. He would have told us if anyone else was coming to look. And we don't want to seem too eager. I want him to come down fifty bucks on the price."

"But Dad—"

"Erin want her wossie?" Mike inquired. Erin had called horses "wossies" when she was a baby. She glared at him.

"Cut it out, Mike," Mr. Calahan said. He turned on the radio and put plates in the dishwasher as he listened to the news. Mike started to look at a car magazine, and Erin went to her room.

Erin's room wasn't much for frills. There was a green-ribcord spread on the bed, a big Sam Savitt poster of all the horse breeds on the wall above it, a complete paperback set of all the Black Stallion stories on the bookshelf, and a herd of Breyer model horses, small ones collected over a dozen birthdays and Christmases, on the dresser. Erin sat on the edge of the bed, tugged off her riding boots, and rubbed the brown leather dreamily. Mike wasn't allowed in her room. It was her own, and she felt safe there with her horse thoughts.

Mike came down the hallway and stopped at her door. "Play you a game of Parcheesi," he offered.

Erin shook her head.

"Monopoly, then."

Worse yet. "I've got homework to do," Erin said.

"After you're done."

"I've got lots," Erin lied.

"Sure you do!" said Mike acidly. "Jeez, have I got a weird sister! All the time stuck in your room. Why don't you come out once in a while? You don't have any friends—"

"Weird yourself! Just scram!"

"Michael," Don Calahan hollered down the hallway, "let her alone!"

Mike left Erin's doorway, but went to his father to argue the point. "She is. She's weird! Keeps to herself all the time."

"Just let her be." Mr. Calahan sounded tired.

"But she acts stuck up."

"Erin is shy. I'm glad you're concerned, Mike, but you can't force a shy person to be friendly." The voices faded away as Mike and his father walked down the stairs to the basement TV room.

Left to herself, Erin remembered for a moment how, years back, she had been afraid of her new two-wheeled bike for months. Her parents had given up coaxing her, but Mike had teased and dared her into learning to ride it. Now she rode a bike daily to Mrs. Bromer's. She scowled, unwilling to be grateful to Mike for anything, and made herself stop thinking of him.

She did her homework, always left until Sunday evening over the weekend. Then she went to bed early and lay awake as she liked to do, daydreaming. She focused a picture in her mind of the gray mare. . . . Silver Girl? Gray Swan? Silky, Princess, Pretty Lady. . . . The daydream image of the mare wavered hazily, seeming even larger than life, strange, almost scary, terribly exciting, terribly— true. That real, exact mare, with all her beauty and faults, would maybe be her own. She was afraid the vet would find her unsound. She was afraid the owner would sell her before her father called. With an aching in her chest she wanted her.

Later, dozing off to sleep, she dreamed of her riding lessons on old William. Learning how to sit deep and relaxed in the saddle at the walk, jog, and canter; how to post to the trot and change leads; how to use her legs and ride without stirrups to improve her seat. William was a generous horse and did everything she asked of him politely. But he was not her horse, and Erin knew it. He moved like a robot under her, a push-button horse, and only when Aunt

Lexie spoke to him did a spark of life come into him. Erin would feel the difference, and for a moment she would tingle with joy—then it would be gone, making her long for a horse of her own, a horse to be all hers, heart and will. A horse that would look to her as William looked to Aunt Lexie. A horse that would nuzzle her and put grass-green kisses on her shirt. A horse that would whinny when she came near and stretch its head toward her to greet her.

Chapter Two

Erin knew she shouldn't, that nothing really was settled yet, but she couldn't help it, she was so full of thoughts of the gray mare. Even though she didn't usually say much to the kids at her bus stop, she had to tell them her news, first thing in the morning.

"I might be getting a horse of my own," she said to no one in particular, since she had no special friend. The older kids ignored her, as she knew they would. And Mike had gotten Mom to drive him to school, thank goodness. But a few of the kids her own age, the seventh and eight graders, clustered around her, interested. All girls, of course.

"She's pretty," Erin told them. "She's sort of white with this kind of gray mane and tail."

"What's her name?"

"Bianca. I mean, that's what it is now. I might name her something neater."

"What kind is she?"

"No special kind. Just a grade horse." How to explain that? "A—horse to ride. . . . "

"You really got a horse? When did you get her?" It was Mikkie Orris, a red-headed girl, butting in.

"I just said I *might* get her. It all depends."

"On what? Your mom and dad?" There was a rapid-fire, smarting-off discussion of parents, with much giggling. Erin stood through it impatiently. She had never been much for giggling.

"Where will you keep her?" It was Marcy Gilmore, an athletic-looking blond girl who lived at the far end of the development from Erin.

"At Mrs. Bromer's."

Several faces turned toward Erin curiously. "How did you ever get in good with the old bag, anyway?" a girl asked her.

"I—don't know. I just hung around. . . . "

Though she could not describe it, she remembered the day as if it were suspended in Lucite to keep on her bookshelf. Last summer. She had ridden her bike up the road and watched the colts for hours, the shiny, up-headed Morgan colts frisking with one another and then sleeping in the sun. And she had watched the broodmares grazing. At last, hesitantly, she had wandered down the lane toward the stable. She knew the rules: Don't touch the horses, don't even come close to them, don't startle or upset them in any way. Mrs. Bromer would not drive a child away without reason, but she did not exactly make children welcome, either. Few of the kids from the development bothered to come here more than once or twice.

Erin drifted in like a shadow at the big door of the stable.

Mrs. Bromer was there, dark as a gnome in the dim light, cleaning out stalls. She was a stocky woman with creased, leathery-looking brown skin and iron-gray hair that she wore in a shapeless mass of frizz. She was wearing snaggled old polyester pants and duck boots, hefting a manure fork, and she turned on Erin with a hard stare.

"You know the rules? Don't touch the horses."

Erin nodded.

"They're all out right now, anyway. What do you want in here?"

"I just—want to watch. . . . "

Mrs. Bromer turned back to her work.

"If I got a horse," Erin blurted, "could I keep it here?"

Mrs. Bromer straightened up again to stare at her. Erin could feel herself shrinking back. She had not known she was going to ask that question until it was out of her mouth. If she had thought about it, she might not have found the nerve.

"Every time I ask my mom and dad for a horse," she explained in a small voice, "they say we don't have any place to keep it."

"What do you want with a horse?" Mrs. Bromer asked sharply—but, then, she always sounded sharp.

"To—to ride!" It seemed like a silly question, until Erin remembered that she had never seen Mrs. Bromer ride her horses.

"Anyone ever teach you how to ride?"

"No—no, ma'am."

"Huh. Well, you ought to know what you're doing before you go getting on a horse." Mrs. Bromer stabbed her manure fork hard into the litter of the stall. She glared at Erin. "Old William and I, we'll teach you how to ride."

Erin did not know whether to take this as a threat or the promise of an incredible gift. "Who's William?" she managed to ask.

"My old gelding. Steadiest horse you're ever likely to ride. Had him since . . . " Mrs. Bromer shook her head, an odd expression on her face, and turned her back. Walking away, she paused, glanced over her shoulder, and jerked her head at Erin. "This way."

Erin followed her. Mrs. Bromer walked fast for an old woman, leaning forward, swinging her arms and puffing. She took Erin down the long lane that ran between pastures and paddocks to the small paddock nearest the woods, farthest from the road. There she leaned on the brown post-and-rail fence.

"WILL-yum!" she called.

A big red roan horse, swishing flies and dozing in the shade at the far side of the paddock, roused and turned his head to look at her. Did she really mean him? Yes, she did. William plodded toward them.

"He's not a Morgan," said Erin in surprise. She

had thought all of Mrs. Bromer's horses were Morgans.

"You're right, he's not. He's the first one I got after— Well, who told you the others were Morgans?"

Erin blinked. "I just knew. The way their necks shoot straight up from their shoulders, and their tails are so thick."

"Huh. Well, what breed do you think William is?"

The gelding didn't look like a purebred horse at all. He was loafing, his head swinging at shoulder level as he walked slowly closer. But he seemed to have a good bit of muscle on him in spite of his lazy way of going. "Quarter horse?" Erin guessed.

"Probably has a lot of quarter horse in him. Most horses around here do." William reached the fence at last, stuck his nose over, and was rubbed hard on the cheekbones and upper neck by his mistress. "He's just a grade horse. Old sweetheart. Dead safe. Must be twenty-five years old by now." Mrs. Bromer sounded faintly surprised.

Erin noticed with a small shock that the soft flesh of the horse's muzzle was creased and wrinkled with age, just like Mrs. Bromer's brown arm. She almost reached out to pat, but remembered the rule in time.

"May I—touch him?"

"Certainly. If you're going to learn to ride on him, you're going to have to touch him, aren't you?"

Erin stroked William's nose and cheeks, breathing in the good horse smell but still half afraid, confused by Mrs. Bromer's harsh way of giving favors.

"But not unless I'm with you," the woman added sternly, as if she had just remembered the rule herself. "That's all, William." She sent the horse away with a swat. Erin followed her back to the stable.

"You'll learn to ride English," Mrs. Bromer told her, making it sound like some sort of decree. "Only type of saddle I can lift anymore."

Erin nodded.

"You'll need leather boots or shoes with hard soles and proper heels. Can't ride in sneakers. Your feet slip through the stirrups, you're in trouble." Mrs. Bromer gave a hard glance at Erin's feet. Erin looked down in turn at her own snub-toed running shoes, feeling suddenly awkward in them, and nodded again.

"Have your mother or father come see me. All right, child, now run along. I have work to do."

Erin took her at her word and ran all the way back to where she had left her bike.

That evening at supper she was so nervous she could not eat. Her parents were tired from their jobs, and Erin knew it would be a good idea if she let them eat and relax before she told them her tremendous news. But she was so excited and terrified she felt sick. After her mother had told her twice, between bites, to eat her steak before it got cold, she put down her knife and fork and gave Erin a long, seeing stare.

"What in the *world*," asked Mrs. Calahan, "is the matter?"

"I— Well, I—" Erin took a deep breath. "I talked with Mrs. Bromer today."

Mr. Calahan also laid down his fork and stared, and Mike gave a hoot of laughter.

"*You* went up to Old Baggy Bromer?"

"Quiet, Michael," Mr. Calahan snapped.

"And I asked her," Erin went on, breathless, being purposely vague about what it was that she had asked, "and she said, well, she would teach me to ride. She said one of you should come talk to her about it."

"I don't *believe* this!" It was Mike again. Don and Tawnya Calahan scowled him into silence, then sat frankly gaping at their daughter. Quiet and shy as she was, Erin had not often surprised them.

"You and Mrs. Bromer discussed the possibility of riding lessons?" Mr. Calahan asked at last.

Erin nodded.

"Well. If you could talk to her, I suppose we can do the same. Right, Tawn?" Don Calahan glanced at his wife and saw that she agreed. "Who should tackle her? You or me?"

"I guess I will." Erin's mother turned back to her steak, but suddenly she, too, seemed not very hungry.

She telephoned Mrs. Bromer while her husband washed the pots and pans. Erin dried, jiggling her legs and trying not to look as if she was listening.

"Hello, Mrs. Bromer? This is Mrs. Calahan, Erin's mother—"

"The little dark-haired girl? That's her name?" Mrs. Bromer's voice knifed clear across the room. "Drat it, I said come on down here and talk to me about her. I hate trying to settle anything on the phone."

"I just wanted to find out when— Right now? In the stable? All right, I'll be there in a few minutes."

Tawnya Calahan left, looking dazed. Erin watched a summer rerun on TV, went to her own room for a while and tried to read, gave it up, and sat in the living room, where she could hear the car pull into the driveway, waiting for her mother's return. Her bedtime came and passed, and her father looked at her, shrugged and said nothing, letting her stay up. Mike phoned to say he was spending the night at a friend's.

At twenty minutes past eleven Mrs. Calahan came in, got herself a glass of iced tea, and sank down wearily in her favorite lounge chair.

"So what's the story?" Don demanded. Erin was afraid to speak.

"It seems," said Mrs. Calahan, word by word, enjoying herself, "that Mrs. Bromer has taken a, well, an interest in Erin. She's got no use for most of the youngsters, she says. They barge in, make noise, act as if they own the place, don't know puppypiddle about horses. That's what she said," Tawnya Calahan added as her husband gave her a startled glance. "But she says she's had her eye on Erin. Says she can tell the young lady has a real love of horses."

Erin was glad her brother was not there to hear that. He would have fallen over from laughing. Mr. Calahan merely chuckled. "That's an understatement," he said.

"I told her I believed she was right. Then I asked something about her horses, to be polite—" Mrs. Calahan sighed. "And she talked and talked, and took me from stall to stall, and I don't remember or understand half of what she said. Then she sat me on a cot in the little room off the stable and talked some more. The gist of it was that she's willing to give Erin riding lessons on that old horse of hers, and she says it's entirely safe. Says she'll supply a hunt cap, that's a sort of hard hat, if it fits Erin, and all the necessary gear except boots. And she doesn't want to charge us."

Mr. Calahan raised his eyebrows. "We really ought to give her something."

"I tried to tell her that, but she's got her own ideas. She says if she gave lessons for money, as if it were a business, it would cause her trouble. She feels she would have to give them to any kid who asked. And she just wants to give them to Erin."

Tawnya Calahan looked at her daughter thoughtfully.

"She wants you to come up as often as you like, to help her around the stable. She says you might want to help her take down the stalls, whatever that means. Says it gets her in the back."

Erin nodded.

"And she also said," Mrs. Calahan told her daughter, "that what you really asked her was, if you were to get a horse, could you keep it at her stable."

"*Ohhhh*," exclaimed Mr. Calahan. "I *see*."

Stung, Erin spoke up, "Well, whenever I asked if I could have a horse, you always said there was no place to keep it!"

"Better just go with the lessons for right now, Squirt." Mr. Calahan was grinning, and Erin scowled as always when he grinned and called her Squirt. Mrs. Calahan got up, yawning.

"Past time you were in bed."

Erin stopped scowling. "Can I go to Mrs. Bromer's tomorrow?"

"I suppose. Just make sure you eat a good breakfast. You're so thin, it'll be a wonder if you can manage a horse."

Erin recognized this as another of her mother's ploys to make her eat, and said nothing.

She went to Willow Hill Farm the next morning, early, in her jogging shoes, because she had no boots yet. And Mrs. Bromer started her on ground work, teaching her how to lead and groom. "Taking down" the stalls turned out to mean shoveling them out entirely and putting in fresh bedding, which was done once a week. Between times they were "picked" with a manure fork. Erin went every day, learning how to clean stalls, how to act around the horses, how to give water, how to put on a halter. And when the leather boots had been bought, a paycheck of her mother's later, her horseback lessons on old William had begun.

"Will-YUM!" Mrs. Bromer had shouted sternly when the old horse failed to respond to Erin's fumbling signals, and the gelding had goggled at his mistress—did she really mean it? He was to obey this Other? Yes, she really did. He moved off with a deep sigh, and Mrs. Bromer drilled Erin until she was dazed. There were basic rules to be learned until they became instinct, and many of them. Heels down. Head up. Take care of trouble before it happens— though there was very little trouble in William. Never hold on by the reins. Sit deep. Feet centered under the body for balance. Never give grain to an over- heated horse. Or water. And many more rules. Erin gave them silly imaginary numbers—rule number eleventy-six, "Never Walk Behind a Nervous Horse," and so on. This was her private joke, and it made her feel better. She did not like Mrs. Bromer much those days, but that didn't matter—just being around the horses was enough, just learning to ride was more than enough for the time. She did everything Mrs. Bromer said and never talked back—she would not have dreamed of talking back.

And sometime in the autumn Mrs. Bromer had said, "You may call me Aunt Lexie."

And sometime in the late winter, when half a dozen of the broodmares were huge with foal, she had said, "Time to start looking for a horse of your own."

Standing at the school-bus stop, Erin said aloud, "I have to really talk with my parents. I mean, they have to pay for the horse and the board money for Mrs. Bromer and everything."

"How come Old Lady Bromer never rides herself?"

"Huh? Oh." Erin blinked at the small group of her classmates clustered around her. "It's her back. She hurt it, falling off a mean horse, years ago. She landed on a sharp rock. So now she just raises the colts and trains them with the driving reins."

"When you get your horse," said Marcy Gilmore, "can we come see it?"

"Can we ride it?" asked Mikkie Orris.

Hope had made her reckless. "Sure," she said grandly.

When she got her horse. When. Oh, when.

Chapter Three

The vet said he might get out to see the mare on Thursday, or, if not, then the first of the next week. It was foaling time. Calls that were not emergencies sometimes had to wait. Erin felt as if she herself might soon become an emergency. Her mother said she was more of a headache than she had been since her terrible twos. Sometimes her parents yelled at her, more often rolled their eyes and let her alone. Shut in her room, she would do drawing after drawing of the mare, drawings of a pretty white horse with finely pricked ears and a charcoal-gray nose, drawings of a neat, compact little horse with a long, full tail shading from white to gray.

Aunt Lexie had little time for her. Five mares had foaled within the past ten days, and Aunt Lexie was tired and grouchy from nights spent on the cot in the tack room. Erin continued coming to the farm every day, helping with the routine work, looking at the foals lying with their mothers in the big, deeply bedded box stalls. Sometimes Aunt Lexie would let her handle one of the week-old ones, stroke it and coax it to follow, pick up the tiny hooves. But most of the time she was on her own. She rode William when it wasn't raining, once up along the road, more often down the lane and into the woods. Riding William was like riding a rented horse. She was only a passenger to him.

She wanted her own horse. Snowbird? Cinderella? Shady Lady . . . Moon Dream . . . None of the names seemed to fit.

The phone rang on Monday night, a week after Erin had ridden the mare. Mrs. Calahan answered it, but Erin could tell at once that it was Aunt Lexie— the older woman's voice crackled out, as always.

"Vet called," she heard Aunt Lexie say. "Mare's sound. Shall I go for her tomorrow?"

Erin was capering around the room in silent agony. "You'd better," said Mrs. Calahan dryly.

"All right. Tell that girl not to expect to hop on her right away. And not to bring a swarm of kids over to see her either." Aunt Lexie hung up, abruptly, as always. Tawnya Calahan turned to her daughter.

"She says tell you—"

"I heard," Erin interrupted. "Yaaah-hooo!" She ran out into the yard and turned several cartwheels.

School the next day seemed endless. Usually a good student, Erin was corrected by her teachers several times for daydreaming. She wanted to revert to her kindergarten habit of chewing her hair, but it was cut too short to reach her mouth, so she chewed her sleeve instead. She did not say anything about the horse to her friends—she was not to bring a swarm of kids, and they were not real friends, anyway, none of them special, just the kids she knew. But she jittered all day, and on the bus, at last going home, she could barely sit still. Coming up to Mrs. Bromer's—

"Is that your horse?" Marcy Gilmore exclaimed,

leaning across the aisle to speak to her.

Erin jumped up, disobeying bus rules for the first time in her life. A white horse with dark points was standing in the small canter ring near the stable. There was an uproar from the eighth graders within earshot.

"Is that him?"

"Oh, wow!"

"He's fat!"

"*She!*" Erin had to shout to make herself heard above the racket. "She's a mare!"

"How about a ride?"

"How about it? Today?"

"No." But they hadn't heard her, or were ignoring her. "Mrs. Bromer says not today," she tried again.

At the mention of Old Baggy Bromer everyone quieted somewhat. "Can we at least come and see her?" Marcy Gilmore asked.

"Not today," Erin said, then remembered that she had promised them all that they could come and see and ride her horse. "Maybe someday soon," she mumbled, and tore away as soon as she got off the bus at the Terrace Heights stop.

Moving at Saturday-morning-cartoon speed, she let herself into the house with the key she always wore around her neck, dumped her books, and ran out to the garage. That morning she had made sure to wear her jeans to school, so there was no need to change clothes. Before the bus was out of sight, and before most of her friends had reached their houses, she was on her bike and pedaling hard toward Willow Hill Farm.

Bianca was every bit as pretty as Erin had remembered her. Puffing, Erin let her bicycle flop in the grass and leaned against the boards of the canter ring, calling to her. The mare paid no attention. Head high, eyes wide and showing their whites, she bugled a long, loud neigh out over the fields of this place that was strange to her. Then she trotted around the ring with short, choppy strides, stood still, and neighed again. Erin saw that her nostrils were flared into large ovals and she was all shiny with sweat, even her legs. Aunt Lexie came out of her house and walked over to stand beside Erin, looking tired.

"They must never have trailered her anywhere. She went in, no problem, but once we were moving she about kicked the trailer to bits. Got herself all in a lather. I've been trying to cool her off for a couple hours. Had a blanket on her for a while, walked her for a while, but she just keeps carrying on."

"Here, girl," Erin coaxed again, holding out a handful of lush spring grass, but the mare did not even look at her.

"You heave the water bucket out of her stall," Aunt Lexie said, "and I'll put her in there and she'll calm down after a while. No use trying to do anything with her today."

Aunt Lexie could not lift the heavy, full bucket herself because of her back. Erin wrestled it off its hook, and Aunt Lexie put the mare into the dim, quiet stall. She and Erin stood watching for a while as the mare explored around and around the sides of the box, snuffling, blowing through her nostrils with a startling noise, pawing and fussing.

"Don't you figure on riding her for at least a week," said Aunt Lexie, "till she gets used to it here."

The mare flung her head up and whinnied, her nostrils moving like a beating heart.

"And don't let anyone else on her," Aunt Lexie added, "not ever, not unless you've got one doozy of a good reason."

"Huh?"

"Don't let anybody else ride your horse. It's up to you to take care of her, do what's best for her. Somebody gets on her that doesn't know what they're doing, somebody with hard hands or some fool who wants to ride like a cowboy, they can really mess her up. Break your heart." There was an edge to Aunt Lexie's tone, as if to say, "I found out the hard way."

"Oh."

"People say they can ride, and they really don't know diddlypoop."

Silence for a while.

"It's a big responsibility having a horse," Aunt Lexie added.

Erin felt some new emotion that was both gentle and fierce. "Well, they can all just stay away," she said softly. "She's *my* horse."

"That she is, kiddo."

Pawing, the mare wobbled her knees, dropped to the stall floor and rolled over on her back with a heave, coating her sticky body with sawdust. Aunt Lexie nodded and gave a satisfied grunt. "Huh. She'll settle down now. Stay if you want, but let her alone. Don't give her water or anything to eat except maybe some hay. I'll take care of her later. Got to go make supper."

The old woman went into her house, leaving Erin in the barn with her new horse.

Erin pushed a mounting block over to the stall and stood on it so that she could see better. Silently she watched. Little by little the mare quieted, accepting the stall as a safe place. Her nostrils stopped fluttering, went back to their normal size and shape. Her ears relaxed, and she stood still, with her head dropped to chest level, resting.

Erin went and got a flake of hay from the end of the bale, took a handful of it, and offered it to the mare, reaching through the stall oars. "Here, girl," she called. "Come here, nice babe."

The mare looked at her for only a moment, and did not move.

Erin opened the stall door and put the hay in the net, then closed and latched the door. Once the girl was out of her stall, the mare came over to eat. Erin watched through the bars as Bianca munched her hay. The horse did not yet seem real to her. As if trying to bring a hazy daydream into focus, she noticed details. Part of the mare's deerlike beauty, she saw, was because of areas of dark skin all around her eyes. Charcoal-gray eyelids blended into her white face, almost as if she were wearing makeup. But no mascara—Erin saw with a small shock that the mare's eyelashes were pure white and very long, curling far out over her large eyes.

"Snowflake," Erin muttered. "Ivory. Gray Lady. Gypsy Girl. Snow Queen. Ermine White. Twilight."

She had read somewhere that the Indians said, or the Gypsies or somebody, that a horse wasn't really your own until you had given it a new name. But no name she could think of seemed good enough. She loved horse names, loved to look at the names in horse magazines, loved the names Aunt Lexie gave her colts and fillies—even though most of them meant nothing to her. Go Back, Pandora's Pride, What the Heck, Scalawag's Revenge, Son of a Gun, Amy My Heart, Knock 'Em Out. But those were names for registered horses. Once given, they were never changed, and the horse was always its own animal, or so it seemed to Erin. She had heard of registered horses that different people rode at the horse shows, like passengers. Good thing Bianca was not a registered horse. She was more like an Indian pony or a Gypsy mare, a horse that could be made her own with the proper name.

"Misty. Snowdrift. Snow Rose, Snowdrop, Lily White—yuck. Ummmm . . . Dusky, Pretty Girl, Queen of Sheba, Cleopatra, Crazy Daisy— Oh, gross. I give up."

Softly Erin got down off her mounting block and opened the stall, slipped in. She knew she was supposed to let the horse alone, but there was something she had to do while Aunt Lexie was not looking. She had also read somewhere that the Gypsies said the best way to make friends with a horse was to blow into its nostrils, the way horses themselves greeted one another. She was a stranger to the mare. She had to trade her scent with the new horse.

Busy at her hay, the mare let her approach. Her head was just about at Erin's head level. Erin puffed softly into the dark paisley shape of the nearest nostril, and Bianca snorted as if hay dust had tickled her. Nothing else happened.

After waiting awhile, Erin sighed and went out.

She double-checked to be sure the stall was latched. " 'Bye, girl," she said. "I have to go home for supper."

The mare did not look at her.

"Well, 'bye," Erin said, and she left the stable, very slowly.

She said nothing at home—Erin generally expected her parents to read her mind. But she was silent at supper that evening, and did not eat well. Her parents looked at her curiously. After all the uproar of the past week, they had been hoping for some happy smiles.

"So, how's the horse?" Mr. Calahan asked at last.

They had noticed. About time. Erin was often disappointed when no one noticed her silences. "Okay," she said dully, meaning "terrible," and her father's eyebrows shot up.

"You don't *like* her now?"

"She doesn't like me! She hates being at a new place, and she hates me. For bringing her there."

"Jeez," Mike said scornfully. His mother glared at him to shush him.

"Erin," said Mrs. Calahan, "she can't possibly hate you. She doesn't even know you. She's just upset."

"I guess," Erin muttered.

"She'll get over it soon."

"She needs a new name," Erin said.

Her mother looked puzzled. "A new name? I think

Bianca is a pretty name. It means white in Spanish."

Erin shrugged. The name Bianca meant nothing to her.

"Wouldn't it be easier on the horse to keep the same name?" her father asked.

She shrugged again, picked up her fork and started eating so that they would not ask her any more questions. It was no use trying to explain to them how a new name changes the luck of the horse.

After supper and clearing away, Erin went into her room to do homework. She could have done it at the dining room table, where she had more space, but she always did it in her room. Math, civics, world history, yuck. Once done, Erin stretched out on her bed with her new library book. Since she had already read every horse book in the school library at least three times, she had found herself a different sort of animal book, one about wolves. About a kingly male wolf and his nearly pure-white, playful mate . . . her fur flying like spindrift. . . .

Erin sat up abruptly, staring. What did that mean? It was a beautiful word.

She left her book and went out to the tall bookshelf in the living room to use the dictionary. Then, taking the stairs with a marching step, she went down to the basement TV room where her family was gathered.

"Spindrift," she told them. "Her name is Spindrift."

"Huh?" They all three blinked at her, taking a moment to come out of the show and see her, and a moment longer to understand that she was talking about her horse.

"Oh," said Mr. Calahan finally. "Spindrift? What does that mean?"

Mike, a high school sophomore, crazy about cars and in a sweat to get his learner's permit the instant his sixteenth birthday arrived, jumped up to show them. "It means she drifts into a spin! Yowwwmmm!"

"It means," said Erin coldly, "the white spray on the tops of waves. Like during a storm, on the ocean."

"Uh-huh," said Mr. Calahan. "Sit down, Mike." His eyes were already fixed blankly back on the TV screen.

"It's a lovely name, hon," Tawnya Calahan said.

Erin went back up to her room, sat at her desk, and wrote the name several times on a piece of paper. Spindrift. It was a wonderful name, and it would make her horse hers, all hers. Her friend of friends.

Who needed regular friends? she thought fiercely, remembering Mike's comment that she had none. Her horse would be better than any human friend. Spindrift would carry her through wilderness at a tireless gallop, jump rivers, rescue her from forest fires. . . .

Thinking faded into daydream as Erin got ready for bed.

"At least she came out of her burrow long enough to tell us the horse's name," Don Calahan remarked to his wife after Mike and Erin were asleep. Sitting by the fireplace late at night, they both felt relaxed. It was a good time to talk.

"Are you comparing our daughter Erin to a mole?" Tawnya gave her husband an amused glance.

"More like a scared rabbit. Good grief, what does she think we're going to do to her if she talks with us?"

Erin's mother said, "I guess we shushed her too much when she was little. We were used to Mike." Both parents smiled, remembering. Mike had always shouted out whatever he was thinking, and as often happens, their younger child had turned out to be just the opposite.

"It's not just us," Mr. Calahan pointed out. "She's shy with everybody. But talk about horse crazy. Then she goes and makes friends with Mrs. Bromer, of all people."

"That's what I keep telling you," Tawnya said. "If the horse doesn't bring her out of her shell, nothing will."

"Well, I hope it works. . . . She's still off in dreamland half the time."

"Give it a chance."

"Yeah, I know. She does seem to be a little more willing to speak up, at least about the horse." Don Calahan stood up, yawning. "Let's get to bed."

"Don, if she does start to open up," Tawnya told him, "let's make sure we don't squelch her."

"Good grief." Mr. Calahan stared sleepily at her. "What do you expect, she'll grow fangs or something?"

"I'm not sure."

Chapter Four

"What are you going to call her for a barn name?"
Aunt Lexie asked. "Spinner? Spindly? The poor
thing."

Erin stared. "Why does she need a barn name?"

"She'll end up with one, you wait and see. No
problem for me—I'll just call her Babe." Aunt Lexie
called half her horses either Babe or Boy. "Come
on, Bianca—Spindrift, I mean. Let's see if we can
get you groomed."

Erin had been saving her allowance for weeks, and recently she had spent it, knowing that her horse would come with nothing but the halter on its head. Laid out along Spindrift's stall ledge were dandy brush, body brush, soft brush, shedding comb, currycomb, and hoof pick. Aunt Lexie brought the mare out of the stall and cross-tied her in the aisleway, where she stood with sawdust and the sweat of yesterday's lathering dried on her, making her hair lie in coarse clumps. Erin picked up her new currycomb.

"Let her sniff it before you touch her with it," said Aunt Lexie.

Erin did. Spindrift blew suspiciously at the currycomb.

"Doesn't look like they ever did much with her," Aunt Lexie added. "Even that currycomb might be strange to her. Move slowly and try not to scare her."

Erin stepped behind the cross ties, standing close to the mare's body, so as not to be injured by a kick, and began to work, moving the currycomb in circles to loosen the dried sweat and dirt. She rubbed very gently at first, and then, as Spindrift seemed not to mind, harder.

"There," said Aunt Lexie, sounding relieved. "She's a good girl, after all." She got her old black-leather-bound record books from the tack room and sat on the bench just outside the stable door, bringing them up to date.

Erin let Spindrift sniff the dandy brush, then swept away the loosened crud with it, starting at the upper neck and working her way to the hindquarters. The body brush came next, to take away more. Erin had to knock a load of dirt loose from it every half minute or so. Then the soft brush, for the face and legs and to put a finer shine on the body. With the dandy brush again, standing to one side, Erin brushed the long, coarse tail.

"There's all sorts of colors in it," she said dreamily. Aunt Lexie, hearing her, snorted softly, a cranky, contented sound. Spindrift liked being groomed. She had relaxed almost to the point of dozing, standing with one hind foot drawn up a little and her hip sagging. Erin was humming to herself. She laid a forearm along the mare's neck so as not to irritate it when she brushed the mane. Like the tail, Spindrift's mane had white hairs and black in it, and gray, yellow, and a few that were reddish brown. Erin counted the colors. She studied the patterns of hair growth, like frost on a windowpane, the whorls and wheat ears along Spindrift's crest and under her throat. She brushed the long cat hairs, winter growth, that made a thin beard under the mare's chin. A warm, warm feeling filled her, and she suddenly reached up and rubbed the mare's neck just behind her ears. Horses were supposed to like having their necks and withers rubbed. . . . Spindrift put all her feet down flat and swung her head away as far as the cross ties would allow. Erin stopped humming and let her hand drop to her side.

"She doesn't know you all that well yet," said Aunt Lexie, who seemed to be able to see around corners and out of the back of her head. "Pick out her hooves while she's quiet."

Erin picked the hooves. Not much had lodged in them, as Spindrift was barefoot. The mare's hooves needed trimming, and she would need shoeing before Erin rode her out on the trail, where rocks might crack her hooves.

Using the old towel her mother had given her, Erin washed her horse's eyes and nostrils, then the udder and dock. "Yecch!" she exclaimed, looking at the black flakes on the towel. "They must not have done that very often."

"Probably never," Aunt Lexie agreed. "Did you feel her jump? You want to do that every day for a while, get her used to handling."

"Should I take her for a little walk? Show her the farm?"

"Fine."

Her left hand curled around the chin strap of the halter, Erin unsnapped the cross ties with her right hand and reached for her brand-new nylon lead with the chain end, clipping it in place.

"Wait," said Aunt Lexie. She heaved herself up from the bench, came and unclipped the lead, showed Erin how to run the chain through one side ring, under the mare's chin and snap it onto the ring on the other side. Erin was surprised. She had never led William like that.

"How come?"

"More control. She acts up, you jerk it. It's like the curb chain on a bit, makes her pay attention."

"But—why would she act up?"

Aunt Lexie stared at her as if doubting her intelligence.

"Cripes, Erin, this mare still has a lot of life in her. She's not a deadhead like old William. She's bound to start testing you soon."

"Testing me?" Erin did not like what she was hearing.

"Certainly. You're her new herd leader, aren't you?"

Erin just stared, and Aunt Lexie puffed out her lips in a sigh, reaching for her pipe to chew on. She seldom lit it, and never in the stable, but she sucked on it in moments of stress.

"Now, you've seen the colts in the pasture," she told Erin in I-am-being-very-patient tones, "nipping and kicking each other. Or even the broodmares, carrying on over who gets petted first. They're settling who's the herd leader, who's next, and so on. Well, you have to show, uh, Spindrift that you're her leader."

"You mean—she's going to fight me?" asked Erin, her voice going up high in dismay.

"Not to bite you or kick you, not unless you really spoil her. She'll try to get away with things. A lot like a colt. Or a kid."

"Oh," said Erin in a small voice. But the horse was supposed to be her friend. . . .

"She might try to bull ahead when you're leading her. So give her a yank with the chain and scold her. And she's likely to shy at something, but the chain will make her think twice about that. Go on, now."

Erin led Spindrift out of the stable and down the lane toward the edge of the woods, where old William stood lazing in his paddock. Old William, with his perfect manners and his complete devotion to Aunt Lexie. Erin saw for the first time that such manners and such devotion were the result of years and years of Aunt Lexie's working with him, and she sighed, not liking the thought.

Spindrift was leading perfectly, her head nodding at Erin's shoulder, neither bulling ahead nor dogging behind. Maybe Aunt Lexie was wrong. Maybe the horse would not test her at all. Maybe—

Spindrift saw a patch of tall grass at the end of the lane and rushed ahead. Without having to think, Erin tightened her grip on the lead so as not to lose her horse. The chain drew snug under Spindrift's chin, and Erin remembered what to do next. She gave it a jerk.

"Whoa!" she ordered, pronouncing it "ho," the way Aunt Lexie did. The mare halted, head up and eyes rolling. Keeping the chain tight, Erin went up to her to speak to her, just as she had so often seen Aunt Lexie speak to the colts she trained.

"We go when *I* say so," she scolded. "You want to knock me down? Okay, let's go." She loosened the chain, turned and walked, and Spindrift followed her quietly—for a moment. Erin had to correct her twice more before they finally reached the tasty-looking patch of grass. Once there, Erin let her graze for a while, all the time watching her and thinking hard.

"Very good," said Aunt Lexie when they got back to the barn. She had been keeping an eye on them, it seemed. "The only thing you could have done better when she pushed ahead, Erin, would have been to make her back up a few steps."

"Next time," Erin mumbled. She put Spindrift in her stall—the mare was not to be let out for a few days except in the small canter ring, not until she knew Erin and Aunt Lexie well enough to come to them without much catching. Erin got up on her mounting block to look at her mare.

"She looked scared of me," she said, sounding tired. "I'd almost rather let her do what she wants."

"You can't," said Aunt Lexie, though not sharply at all. She seemed to understand, even, what Erin was saying. "You have to control her. She's bigger than you; she could hurt you if you don't."

"I'm not afraid," Erin said.

"You've never been hurt."

Remembering that Aunt Lexie had been hurt, Erin kept her mouth shut.

"Don't want to be, either. So you have a responsibility. Not only to take care of the horse, but to keep yourself safe, do you see?"

Some response seemed to be expected, so Erin nodded.

"Have to make her mind or she won't be any good to ride," Aunt Lexie added.

Erin was silent. "Can I give her a jelly bean?" she asked finally.

"From your hand? I suppose. She seems mannerly. But if she ever starts to get nippy, you'll have to stop."

"Treats Make a Horse Nippy"—rule number twelveteen.

It took a lot of calling and coaxing before Spindrift would look around at Erin and see the jelly bean. Once she had finally spotted it, she came right over and lipped it off of Erin's palm. Spindrift was not backward where food was concerned. But she turned away sulkily before Erin could pat her.

The horse wasn't going to be her friend right away.

Not for a jelly bean. Not even with her beautiful new name.

Erin stood watching Spindrift silently for a while, struggling with the thought that she was going to have to change her ideas. Finally she said, "Well, I guess I'd better go home."

"We'll turn her out in the paddock Saturday," Aunt Lexie hollered after her, "when you're around. You'll want to see that."

Saturday morning turned out to be gray and cloudy. The sky seemed to be getting darker by the moment, instead of lighter. Erin skipped breakfast, hoping her mother would not notice. She rushed in agony through the chores her parents had assigned her, leaving a trail of forgotten objects behind her for Mike to deal with later—his job was straightening up. Before her family was awake, she was out of the house and on her way to the stable. If the rain would only hold off for just a little while longer—

"She has to finish her *hay*," said Aunt Lexie crankily.

"Can't she come back and finish it later?"

"Well, maybe some of it. But she has to digest her grain. Give the poor creature some time, girl."

The sky was purple-gray, dark as slate, when they

led the mare out at last. Spindrift looked blazing white against the gloomy sky and dark-green grass. She stood for just a moment with her head flung up, nostrils wide open. Then with a deep, chesty whicker and a gigantic thrust of her hind legs, she leaped into a gallop down the center of the paddock.

Erin leaned forward with her mouth open, watching.

The mare shied sharply at the far fence—for sheer fun. No horse had ever looked less afraid. She whirled on her hindquarters and ran alongside the rails, kicking and bucking at every stride, circled the paddock, running past with a noise that magnified in Erin's mind into the rumble and roar of ocean waves. Head high, tail high, Spindrift galloped, white as lightning against the dark sky, white as seething froth, white as a clipper ship's sails—though Erin had never seen such sails—and the hairs of her mane and tail flew like spray. Like spindrift.

"All *right*," Erin breathed.

"She's a proud horse," Aunt Lexie stated, "and a bold horse." The words were not poetry coming from her, but a horsewoman's jargon, words of truth. To Erin, they sounded wonderful.

Spindrift had stopped her bucking and snorting

and shying. She rounded the paddock at a steady gallop, a canter, a trot, then slowed down to a walk and began to explore her paddock by scent, swinging her head low and snuffling along the ground. Erin watched the mare's every move, thrilled. She could not imagine greater perfection than that before her. Spindrift began to paw the grass.

"Upsy-daisy," said Aunt Lexie with a chuckle.

Spindrift went down with a grunt and a surge to roll, came up shaking herself like a huge dog. Erin laughed out loud.

"She's settling in so well," Aunt Lexie remarked, "you might be able to ride her sooner than I said. If you want." She looked down at Erin with crinkling eyes, knowing very well that the girl was dying to ride.

Erin jumped with excitement, then pounced. "When?"

The old woman sucked on her pipe, looking vague and enjoying herself.

"Aunt Lexie, when?" Erin persisted. "Today?"

"Hardly today," said Aunt Lexie dryly. The clouds hung black as a bruise. She and Erin called Spindrift in from the paddock, and within the moment it started to rain.

Chapter Five

"Erin!" her mother shouted as she went to put out the garbage after Saturday lunch. "What is this disgusting object by the back door?"

Erin came running. It was the towel she had been using to clean parts of Spindrift, and her mother was holding it between thumb and forefinger, at arm's length. It was, Erin had to admit, sort of gross.

"I brought it home to get it washed—I mean, to wash it," she said, remembering that she was supposed to take care of the horse laundry.

"Then wash it! Don't leave it lying here. Go put it in right now."

"Okay, okay!"

"And don't put anything else in with it!" Mrs. Calahan yelled after her.

"*Sheesh*," Erin muttered, but not loud enough so that her mother could hear. Though of course she had not told her parents so, it had been a rough week. It was getting harder each day to deal with the kids at school.

"When do we get to come see your horse?" girls would ask her between classes or on the bus. Afraid to simply tell them that they couldn't, Erin had tried all ways of putting them off.

"Soon. She's nervous."

"Maybe tomorrow. She's still settling in."

"Maybe tomorrow . . . "

In the morning, facing school, she had often thought of being sick. Her stomach really did hurt, every day. But she knew that if she was too sick to go to school, she would have to be too sick to go see Spindrift. So Wednesday, Thursday, Friday, she had walked off to the bus stop, very slowly, and made it through another day.

"Maybe tomorrow . . . "

"Maybe next week . . . "

"Next week!" Marcy Gilmore exclaimed on the way home, Friday. "It's getting worse!"

"How about this weekend?" Mikkie Orris put in. "Just to come see."

"How about it?"

Several of them were staring at her. Erin felt cornered and finally came out with the truth.

"You can't. It's bad for the horse."

"How come?"

"She'll get confused. Too many people . . . " Spindrift was not a toy or a game, but a living being that depended on her, Erin, and Erin knew that already, down to her bones. Her feelings told her to protect the horse. But her feelings were hard to explain.

"Aw, maaan, we won't do nothing!"

"You promised!"

"Traitor!"

"Scared of Old Baggy Bromer?" someone jeered.

It would have been easy to blame everything on Aunt Lexie. So easy, Erin grew angry at the thought.

"She's *my* horse, and you're not messing with her!"

"But you *said*—" Marcy Gilmore started.

"I didn't know then!" Erin interrupted her, shouting. Not used to having to speak her mind, she had gotten loud, and she was standing up. "So you can all just stay away!"

"Siddown!" hollered the bus driver.

She sat, feeling anger beating on her. She hunched over with her arms across her chest for protection.

"Erin Calahan," declared red-headed Mikkie, "you are a stuck-up, selfish, ugly brat."

"You're a pig," said someone else.

"More like a dipstick," said a boy who had been listening in, and the group laughed.

"Dipstick!"

"You're a dip, Erin!"

"Ugly!"

"Brat!"

"Pig!"

"Sheesh! Is she ever *weird*."

Ready to cry, but refusing to cry, Erin had run for her house as soon as she was off the bus. A day later, putting the filthy towel in the washer, she seemed still to hear yelling voices inside her head. She had been half afraid that Mikkie Orris and her gang would come by while Spindrift was running in the paddock that morning. But no one had.

Her mother was waiting for her when she came upstairs. Tawnya looked tired. "Now, remember, I have to go to that nutrition seminar this afternoon," she told Erin, "and Mike has practice, and your father has a wedding to shoot. So you're in charge of supper."

Nodding without really hearing, Erin headed out through the garage door to go see Spindrift. Once she was at the stable, nothing would bother her. It was her hideaway, her refuge.

The mare was shedding her winter fur. Hair gathered in white billows on the stable floor as Erin scraped it free with the shedding comb, and the fine, silky summer coat that was growing underneath shone like white water. Erin groomed Spindrift for a long time. In the cool, dim, silent aisleway of the stable, she could forget her mother's tired face, forget the names the kids had called her and the angry sound of their voices. She always forgot everything else when she was with her horse.

Including the time.

She walked the mare, and had a talk with Aunt Lexie, and groomed Spindrift some more. It was very late when she started home. Opening the back door, she expected to smell supper cooking, but instead she came up against her mother's angry stare. Tawnya Calahan was trying not to lose her temper.

"Erin," she said, in her I-will-be-calm-but-firm voice, "you are late. And I must have told you five times to put our dinner in the oven and set the table. You did neither. Now we have to try to make do with leftovers."

The knot in Erin's stomach was back again. "Sorry, Mom," she said. "I forgot."

"Forgot! It's your middle name these days! You have not emptied the dishwasher any day this week. You know you are to empty the dishwasher and set the table when you come home from school. You have not been living up to the agreement we made, and I am beginning to be sorry we ever got you that horse."

"Aw, Mom—" Erin shifted from foot to foot. "Mike should do that stuff sometimes."

"Mike doesn't even get home from practice until dinnertime! If you may have a horse, Mike may certainly have his baseball practice."

"Well, if you didn't have a job, you could do it yourself!"

The temper was lost. "If I didn't have a job," Mrs. Calahan shouted, "you wouldn't have a horse!"

"I'll set the table now," Erin mumbled.

"It's already done. Tomorrow morning, you stay here and do the jobs you have been neglecting. You haven't changed your bed since I don't know when, and it smells like a stable. You haven't cleaned your room or done anything around the house. Every day you leave your books and papers all over the sofa—"

"But, Mom, Aunt Lexie said we're going to saddle Spindrift tomorrow and see if she'll go English!" Erin's voice rose so high it cracked. She had not yet ridden her new horse.

"You can do that in the afternoon."

"It's supposed to rain in the afternoon! Mom, I'll clean my room when I get back. Please. I promise."

Tawnya felt as if her head would split. Seeing the look on Erin's face, she would have liked to have given in to her, but temper would not let her. And fair was fair.

"I've heard that before. You stay here until you've done your share."

Erin felt her face flush as red as Mikkie Orris's hair, and she gave up on holding back tears. "I hate you!" she shouted at her mother. Then she ran for her room and slammed the door.

Supper was silent, the evening uneasy. Tawnya took two Excedrin and went to bed half an hour early. She had decided to get up much earlier than she usually would on her Sunday off, hoping to have her daughter out of the house by ten. No breakfast, she thought wearily, and she set her alarm for seven.

Sometime before daybreak her rest was disturbed by a dull humming sound. Mrs. Calahan hung on to sleep for a while longer, but in the end she sat up in bed, groggy but awake. She felt her way into her big, soft slippers and padded down the hallway in search of the noise. Funny, the living room lights were on. Who . . .

Erin.

She was in there, running the vacuum cleaner, down on her hands and knees with her skinny hind end in the air, fishing things out from under the furniture.

"Erin Laine Calahan!" Tawnya was too startled to be very angry.

Erin came up with a jerk, bumping her head against the coffee table. She rubbed it with her left hand, still clutching the vacuum with her right. She was fully dressed, and by the looks of things had been at work for some time. The tall clock over the fire-place said quarter past six.

"I'm sorry, Mom. I didn't mean to wake you." Erin looked guilty. "Go back to bed."

"I'm *up* now."

"I thought I could get this done early. I've already changed my bed and scrubbed the bathroom, and dusted, and—"

"Turn off the vacuum cleaner," said Mrs. Cala-han, "and go back to bed yourself. It looks as if it's raining, anyway."

Erin gasped and jumped up to look out the picture window. In the pale light before sunrise, big splat-ters of rain could be seen coming down, polka-dot-ting the driveway.

"Oh, no!" Erin wailed. "*Everything* is going wrong lately." From sheer tiredness, she started to sniffle. Sighing, her mother came over and gave her a hug.

"Go back to bed," she ordered, and Erin did.

Shortly after nine Erin was awakened by a gentle shaking. Her mother stood over her.

"It's stopped raining," Mrs. Calahan said.

Erin struggled, getting tangled in the sheets in her hurry to lift the window shade. Outside, grass and leaves were wet, but the sun was shining. Already in her clothes, Erin made a dive for her riding boots.

"All right!" she exclaimed. "I mean—can I go?"

"Yes, you may go. By the way, you did a nice job on the bathroom."

Erin was already out in the garage, getting her bike.

"Just do it in daylight the next time!" her mother yelled after her.

Erin pedaled off at top speed, pretending not to hear.

"Blast," said her mother to herself. "I forgot to make her eat." She stood watching the bike sail away down the road.

Aunt Lexie was working a colt in halter on the driveway, and Erin slowed her bike to a crawl so as not to startle the youngster.

"So there you are," Aunt Lexie remarked. "Sleep in?"

"Sort of. I mean, my mother wanted some help aound the house."

"Huh. Yes, I guess she would, now and then. She should see mine."

Erin smiled. She had been inside Aunt Lexie's home a few times, briefly, and the place was like a jungle. Dirt and clutter, and cobwebs hanging down in loops Tarzan could swing on, fuzzy stuff growing on surfaces like moss. Wild. The tack room in the stable, with its own sink and small refrigerator, its heater, cot, and the framed hunting prints on the walls, seemed far more homelike. It was not hard to tell where Aunt Lexie really lived.

"Ready to ride? We'll try her in the ring."

Not the small canter ring, but the larger training ring behind the stable. Erin went to Spindrift's stall. The mare, as usual, turned her back. But while she refused to come to Erin's call, she could be bribed.

"Come get your oats," Erin told her.

She swung around slowly, came over with supreme slowness and lipped the handful of oats. Erin took hold of her mane with the other hand and slipped the halter on her when the oats were gone. Spindrift swung her head sideways in bored protest.

"Grouchy mare," Erin accused.

She groomed her, and Aunt Lexie brought several saddles. The one that fit William sat up too high on Spindrift, who was rounder. The oldest, most dried-up saddle fit best.

"You take that home and mink oil it," Aunt Lexie ordered.

More work.

The girth was a problem—since Spindrift was so hay-bellied, it had to be very long. Finally Aunt Lexie found one that fit, not a leather one but one made of strands of cotton cord, dusty from being hung on a hook in the loft.

"Don't recall when I got it, or what for," Aunt Lexie muttered with a puzzled look.

Erin buckled it on. She tugged and strained at the billets to pull it tight. This was something she always had to do for herself—Aunt Lexie could not manage it since she had hurt her back.

"Got it good and tight? All right." Aunt Lexie brought a light bridle with a plain eggbutt snaffle. "I don't think she'll need a noseband," she said, more to herself than to the girl. Erin slipped the bit into Spindrift's mouth, and Aunt Lexie showed her how to adjust the cheek straps so that the bit sat correctly in the horse's mouth.

"Just one wrinkle at the corners of her lips. . . . "

Erin led her horse out to the ring, nearly skipping with happy anticipation. Her very own horse to ride. Soon they would be cantering across the countryside. . . .

"Now," said Aunt Lexie, flatly, as she said everything, "you ride at a walk today. Maybe next week we'll try for a trot. You won't get to canter her for a month or two."

Erin gaped. Another dream shattered. "Why not?"

"Because she's not in condition. Yet. Not supple. Or strong. It's dangerous to ride at speed on a horse that's not fit. Next week I'll show you how to longe her up there in the canter ring, and after maybe six weeks of that, three times a week, she'll be ready."

Speechless, Erin pulled her stirrup irons down the leathers and mounted. Spindrift started to move off, then stopped.

"Did you tell her to go?" Aunt Lexie asked.

"No."

"Make her whoa if she walks off. Did you tell her to stop?"

"No."

"Huh." Aunt Lexie gave a puzzled shrug. "Well, get your heels down. Stirrups the right length?"

They were. Erin checked her seat, let her weight settle into the saddle, looked out wide-eyed over white ears. Time to ride. She signaled for the walk.

Spindrift swung her head up and down but refused to move.

"She's balking," Aunt Lexie said. "Strange place, maybe. Try again."

Erin tightened her legs and clicked her tongue to send Spindrift forward. The mare flattened her ears back against her neck and stepped backward.

"Give her a good kick."

Erin did. The mare started forward with a jump, then walked, but her ears were still back, she swished her tail angrily at every step, and Erin could feel how tense she was under the saddle. The walk was stiff and jolting.

"Keep your hands real soft," called Aunt Lexie. "She has to learn she can trust you not to hurt her."

Erin made two circuits of the ring, hoping Spindrift would relax, but if anything the mare grew more nervous. She speeded her walk into a rough, jarring trot.

"I said walk her today!" Aunt Lexie yelled. "Keep her at the walk!"

Erin signaled the mare with her back muscles and gently tightened her reins. Spindrift tossed her head and fussed.

"Keep your hands light!"

"They are," Erin muttered, too softly for Aunt Lexie to hear. Concentrating on following the mare's abrupt movements with her hands, she felt as if she were losing her seat, as if every jolt threatened to throw her off.

"Do some circles!"

Erin pressed with her inside leg and hinted with the right rein, trying to guide her mare in a circle to the right. Spindrift balked, stopping where she was.

"Keep her moving! Use leg!"

Erin tightened her legs on Spindrift, nudged with her heels. Spindrift only rounded her back, bunching to buck. Just as Erin lifted her legs to give a sharp kick, Aunt Lexie shouted again.

"I said use some leg on her!"

"I am!" Erin yelled out loud. She had never shouted at Aunt Lexie before, or so much as answered back, but it had been a hard week. "I am using leg, and I am keeping my hands soft, and I never told her to trot! She's all fussed up! She's about ready to toss me!"

For a moment Aunt Lexie looked shocked and furious. Erin stiffened, certain she was doomed to die. But then, sheepishly, the old woman smiled.

"That's my girl," she said. "When I'm out of line, you stand up to me, Erin." She walked over to the balky mare, took hold of the cheek strap. "Okay, get off her. Something's wrong. We'll have to start over, try another bit, maybe."

They walked back to the stable in silence, with Erin leading Spindrift by the reins. They put the mare between the cross ties, and Aunt Lexie slipped the bridle off the mare, looking carefully at her lips and mouth. "Nothing wrong there that I can see," she said. "You might as well halter her and get the saddle off her. No use riding her anymore today."

Erin did as she was told. "What's wrong with her?" she asked in a small voice.

"Dunno, kiddo. I have to think."

But as the cotton-cord girth fell away from Spindrift's side, a tuft of hair came with it. Erin ran her hand along a raised line, like a welt, on Spindrift's side and belly, and Aunt Lexie whistled.

"Wheeee-oo! So that's it. Son of a gun."

"What happened?" Erin asked, trying to stroke the crimped hairs flat.

"Fold of skin caught between the cords. Stupid me. I just remembered why I stopped using that girth. Try the soft brush, Erin." Aunt Lexie strode off toward her house.

Erin brushed anxiously at the line. There was no

blood or anything like that, not even bare skin that would start a girth gall, but she still felt awful. She thought, I was the one who tightened the girth, I should have noticed. "Poor Spindrift," she said aloud.

After several minutes Alexandra Bromer returned, rolling her eyes. "I was using it as a draft doggie," she said. "Clean forgot what it was for in the first place."

She was carrying something that looked like a piece of bathroom rug.

"Girth cover," she explained to Erin. "Should have thought of it before," she admitted. "You've got a super nice little horse there, kiddo. A lot of them would have reared up under you. Gone over backward, even. The way we had it, that girth pinched her every time she took a step."

"Oh, no!" Erin wailed. "You mean I hurt her the whole time?"

Aunt Lexie gave her a surprised look. "It didn't take us that long to catch on. You're bound to make mistakes, Erin. Only way you learn. Let's get this girth cover on that excuse of a girth and try it again."

The fuzzy piece of cloth Aunt Lexie had brought fit over the girth like a sleeve. Erin saddled and bridled Spindrift again, and this time everything worked nicely. During the next hour, with Erin keeping her hands soft and quiet, Spindrift made a start on learning to relax her jaw, yield on the bit, and respond to English reining.

"She's smart," Aunt Lexie said. "Loads of sense, that horse."

"How's the horse?" Mr. Calahan asked at supper.

"Okay. Aunt Lexie says she has a nice pleasure walk," Erin reported proudly. "Says she might have some Arabian blood in her, as pretty as her head is."

"Uh-huh," said Don Calahan, eating. Arabian blood meant nothing to him.

"She learns fast." Erin gulped a huge forkful of spaghetti.

"Aunt Lexie says we have to have the vet up," she added as an afterthought. "Spindrift needs her teeth floated—that's part of the reason she's not in better shape. And she might as well have her worm shot and her five-in-one shot at the same time."

"Good grief," said her father, looking dazed, understanding none of this except his part in it. "Another bill."

"What do you mean, teeth floated?" asked Mike.

"That's when they file down the sharp edges of the teeth so the horse can chew better."

"Poor horse," Mike sighed. "How did she ever get along without you?"

Erin did not bother to answer or scowl at his teasing tone. She was still astonished that she was alive, that she had talked back and Aunt Lexie had not killed her.

Chapter Six

"How's the horse?"

It was Marcy Gilmore, taking a seat next to Erin on the school bus, Monday morning bright and early. Erin looked at her with a sidelong, uneasy glance, as if she were a shying horse herself. Marcy had been part of that shouting crowd on Friday, had she not? But come to think of it, she had not done any of the shouting that Erin could remember. And she looked friendly.

"Okay," Erin said. "We have to have the farrier out sometime soon."

"The what?"

"The blacksmith. The horseshoer," Erin explained. "I won't be able to ride her much until we do."

And even then, she thought with a pang, only to go around a ring at walk and trot, until Aunt Lexie gave the word. A far cry from her dreams of cantering across the countryside.

"But Aunt Lexie wants to show me how to longe her," she added bravely.

"Lunge her? You mean, make her jump?"

"Nuh-uh. It's when they make the horse go around in a circle, on a long line—"

"Oh yeah." Marcy sounded interested. "I've seen them do that. What's it for?"

"To build up Spindrift's muscle and make her supple. That means make her bend—"

"Spindrift?"

"That's what I named her."

Erin began to feel dizzy with delight. Here, at last, was a person who really wanted to hear about her horse. Really! She could tell. Eyes wide and happy, she settled back and talked about Spindrift.

Marcy nodded and listened and asked questions. When the bus pulled up in front of the school, Erin was still talking and Marcy was still listening.

"Back of the industrial park," Erin was saying, "where it turns to country, there's miles of good riding trails, Aunt Lexie says. Once school's over I'll be able to go riding all day."

The other kids were piling off the bus. Marcy and Erin blinked, and Erin realized that she had been chattering nonstop for almost half an hour.

"Hey," she said lamely as they got up, "it's been nice talking to you."

"I like hearing about horses," Marcy said.

"Well, hey—" Erin followed her off the bus with an armload of books. "I'd like to let you come see her, really I would. But it was dumb of me to say people could ride her, before."

Marcy looked at her with an odd, tight expression on her face. "I wasn't going to ask," she said, and before Erin could say anything, she turned and disappeared into the crowd of kids arriving for school. Erin stood feeling somehow uncomfortable, not wanting to know why.

Nothing was ever simple.

It was a beautiful day, sunny and warm but not too warm, with just enough breeze to keep the flies away, a perfect day for riding. The school hours dragged. Erin chewed on her knuckles and messed up badly on a math quiz. On the bus, going home at last, she tapped her fingers against the window glass as if she could somehow break out and speed to the stable on her own. Marcy was not on the bus, and Erin sat alone.

"Dip!" Mikkie Orris jeered from across the aisle. "Hey, Erin. Are you a dip or a dumbhead?"

Of course there was no answer to that.

"Or a dippy pig?"

"Don't you know?" someone else joined in, as if it were no more than a game. "She's a dipstick!"

Most of the kids were full of spring fever, bored and restless. Delighted with the game, they started a chant.

"Dip-STICK! Dip-STICK! Dip-STICK! Dip—"

"Shaddup!" the bus driver yelled, but they didn't. Not entirely.

Their chanting followed her as she got off the bus at her stop and ran. She always ran, so they did not bother to chase her. Biting her lip, she let herself into the house and watched through the drapes until they were all in their homes. Then she headed off down the road to see Spindrift.

Halfway to the stable she remembered the dishwasher.

"Oh, maaan—" It was a plea to the heavens.

She turned her bike around and tore back home, ran from dishwasher to table and cupboards, found the note her father had left her, and turned the crock pot to high as he had directed. He did most of the meal planning and cooking, as her mother got tired of dealing with food at work. Erin checked to make sure she had remembered everything, then pedaled off at top speed toward Willow Hill Farm.

Aunt Lexie was not there.

Erin could not believe it. She knocked on the house door, even. But Aunt Lexie did not answer, and her Blazer was missing. Though it hardly seemed like her, she must have gone on some errand somewhere.

"Oh, CRUD!"

Erin stood thinking resentfully of all the things that had gone wrong. Parents who wanted dishwashers emptied, and the stupid math quiz, and the kids calling her names, and now Aunt Lexie, not there for her. She felt an urge to run away. She and Spindrift, galloping off into the wilderness . . .

Suddenly she balled her fists and strode down to the stable. If she could not run away, she was going to at least have a real trail ride.

Grooming her mare and tacking her up, Erin felt herself relax, as she always did. Anger trickled away, and a tingle of excitement filled her instead. Dreaming of a canter, wind in her hair, she nearly went without her hunt cap. But then she jammed the silly velveteen-covered thing on her head and buckled the chin strap. Better not be too reckless. She decided against the canter, this time. Just a nice quiet trail ride at the walk. She went over a checklist as she led the mare out.

"Safety bars open? Check." Better to drop a stirrup than be dragged by a runaway, Aunt Lexie said. "Reins straight? Girth tight? Check. Anybody know where we're going? How could they—I don't know myself!" She grinned, full of the spirit of adventure. "Off we go, girl!"

The good, good sound of stirrup irons snapping down their leathers into place. Spindrift moved off while being mounted, instead of standing still as she was supposed to, but Erin didn't care. It felt fine and tall to ride out all alone. Down the lane, along the woods to the path that led through them. Moving along with her face at the level of the opening tree buds, their tiny yellow-green flowers brushing her cheeks, sun warm on her back, the creak of saddle leather and the rocking rhythm of the walk . . . it was a blissful ride. Spindrift's head nodded eagerly, her long mane stirring. Three deer stood back in the woods and watched them pass—Erin would not have noticed them, so still, except that Spindrift raised her head and looked. Then she saw them, every detail, their dark noses and big ears and the red sheen of their springtime coats. They stood and let her study them, not afraid of the horse. And there were birds calling and flying across in front of them, and the star-shaped spring flowers in the grass. Erin felt as if she could see everything for miles. And Spindrift was being an angel. Erin could not imagine what Aunt Lexie had been waiting for.

"*Good* girl," she told the mare, stroking her.

They took the path through the woods behind the development. Mayapple was opening like scalloped umbrellas on the forest floor. Then, along the lawns back of the industrial park. Forklifts were working, and the noise of heavy machinery echoed all around, but it didn't bother Spindrift, Erin was pleased to see. Soon they left that behind. Keeping her to a quiet walk, Erin guided Spindrift along the edge of unfamiliar woods, looking for a path of some sort, a deer trail, maybe. She had to look twice before she found it. No more than a space between the brush and the trees, it led straight into the strange woods. Maybe through them to what lay beyond, farmland and miles of trails . . .

Aunt Lexie said a horse can always find its way home.

Taking a deep breath, Erin sent Spindrift along the vague little path, ducking twigs and branches. Some were so low she had to put her head down beside the horse's neck. The mare went on calmly. There were fallen trees. Spindrift had to step over the trunks. Saplings bent across the path she pushed aside with her chest.

"Attagirl. Super trail horse. Wish the kids could see us—"

Spindrift stopped short, her nose up to scent the air, her ears pricked and twitching. Erin felt the horse's whole body tense up and start to tremble.

Keep a frightened horse moving past whatever scared it. Rule number thousandty-three.

"Come on, Spindrift!"

Erin coaxed with her voice and nudged the mare with her heels. No good. Spindrift stood as stiff as a bronze equestrian statue in some town square, but puffing aloud like a steam engine. Her every muscle was bunched. Erin gave her a sharp kick, and the mare moved, but only to try to turn back the way they had come. Erin held her where she was, wishing she had brought a crop—

There was a noise that seemed to come from everywhere, a rumbling, muttering, growling noise that made the small hairs rise on the back of Erin's neck. And a whinny of terror from the mare, and what seemed to Erin like an explosion under her— Spindrift was rearing, high, straight up in the air, Erin was looking up at branches and sky, the mare was going over backward! There was no time to be scared—Erin knew she had to do something or be crushed. She let go her grip on the reins, kicked her feet out of the stirrups and sailed off to one side. Giddily, in midair, she thought she saw something move in the bushes, just a glimpse of some animal, large, dark, and very furry. Then her back hit the ground, her head hit a tree, and she lay and listened to the sound of Spindrift's frantic hoofbeats fading away toward the barn and home.

No wonder. Couldn't expect any horse to face a bear—

Bear?

It grumbled again, a fierce, throaty noise, and Erin opened her eyes, focused them with an effort.

Yes, it really was a bear, shuffling toward her. From where she lay on the ground it looked huge. Because she was knocked breathless anyway, Erin closed her eyes again and lay still, limp as a dishrag. She could hear the snuffling of the bear, smell its breath as it sniffed her—it had been eating something rotten. It turned her over with a long-clawed paw. Erin let her arms and legs flop lifelessly. Then she felt nothing more. She seemed to hear the bear turn and amble away, but she did not dare to look, or did not have the strength to look, and she fainted.

Some time later, with no idea what time, she awoke, groaned, got up shakily, and trudged off toward home.

It was almost dark as she passed behind the industrial park. Cars along the road between the factories had their lights on. Erin thought of stopping a car and asking for a ride, but she had been warned not to get into cars with strangers, and she was worried about Spindrift. She was determined, silly as it seemed afterward, to get back to the barn and see if the mare was all right. One foot in front of the other . . . the task of walking took all her energy. Past the last factory . . . good. She turned in along the path that came out behind Terrace Heights.

Very dark in the woods. For the first time Erin began to wonder vaguely if she might not be in trouble. Couldn't see to follow the path . . .

Wait. Flashlights ahead.

"Erin!" called a man's voice, her father's voice, sounding high, hoarse, and scared. "Erin!" A woman's old, husky voice, Aunt Lexie's.

"Here," she muttered, then realized they would not be able to hear her. Funny, it was hard to shout. "Here!" she called, and they came crashing toward her, the beams of their flashlights bouncing wildly. As soon as they spotted her their fear gave way to a torrent of anger.

"Erin!" bellowed her father. "Where the devil have you been!"

"Can't a person go get her back fixed—" That was Aunt Lexie.

"We've been looking for you for hours!"

"—without you going off without a word—"

"Don't you ever do that again!"

"—not even a note. Don't you know how to use pencil and paper, girl?"

"You're going to be grounded."

"Now my back's worse than ever."

"Your mother's out driving around in the car, looking for you. . . . "

Erin paid no attention to most of this, hearing it only foggily. "Is Spindrift all right?" she asked.

"Of course she is!" Aunt Lexie snapped.

"I've had it with that horse!" her father roared. "It's been one thing after another—"

"It was a bear," said Erin.

"—ever since we got her."

"A real bear. Out beyond the industrial park."

"That does it!" Mr. Calahan reached top volume. "The horse throws you, and you expect me to believe it was a bear, built up as it is around here—what sort of an idiot do you think I am? Erin, that is the last straw. First thing in the morning, that horse is going back where we got her!"

Erin could not see him any longer. Her vision had gone black.

"Don't say such a thing, you bully!" she heard Aunt Lexie say. "You'll break her heart!"

"Shut up, you old hag!" Mr. Calahan screamed.

"I am an old *bag*, thank you," Aunt Lexie told him icily.

Seeing no reason to stand up any longer, Erin quietly folded to the ground.

Chapter Seven

Erin kept only hazy memories of her father's gathering her up and carrying her, the ambulance, the bright lights of the emergency room. What he had said—Spindrift to be taken away—she could not face thinking about that. She went to sleep, or fainted again, and refused to wake up. Time after time people would shake her, and she would squirm away from their hands and go back to sleep.

"She's in shock," someone said once, "but she's

not going into a coma. Couple days, she'll be okay."

She finally awoke in the morning to find herself in a hospital room, a pale-colored place, as all hospital rooms seem to be, with her father seated on a chair beside her bed. Mr. Calahan looked very tired. Erin stared at him. Then, remembering what he had said, she turned her face away, too heartsick to speak. Spindrift might already be gone.

"Now wait, hon. I was upset; I said some stupid things." She felt her father lay a hand on hers. "You should know I wouldn't do anything with your horse without discussing it with you first. Erin, look at me."

She faced him, scowling to hide her fear. "Where's Spindrift?" she whispered.

"At Mrs. Bromer's. And we're not going to say any more about it until you're feeling better."

If that was supposed to make Erin feel reassured, it didn't. She stared at her father uneasily. He shifted in his seat and looked down at his hands.

"I'm sorry I thought you were lying to me," he said. "There really was a bear."

Erin accepted the change of subject. "You went to see for yourself?"

"Me? Lord, no. I've been right here all night,

except for when your mother took over. No, Mrs. Bromer called the Forest Service, and they went and spotted the bear. It's in today's paper. Seems it's just a half-grown cub, and the mothers kick them out around this time of year, and they wander. But the state game lands are a good twenty miles from here. First time a bear has been seen around here in thirty-five years."

"Just my luck," said Erin sourly.

"It seems there's some sort of illegal garbage dump down in those woods, and he's been feeding at it."

"A *garbage* dump," Erin groaned. "That does it. I give up." She was feeling light-headed, and for some reason the garbage dump seemed like the last straw.

"You feel okay, Squirt?"

"I have a headache, and I feel sort of woozy."

"I bet. You're on painkillers, and you're supposed to keep very quiet. You have some concussion. That hard hat of yours took the worst of it—dented clear in. After they feed you and the doctor checks you over again, they'll probably send you home."

Tawnya Calahan came in, smiling a greeting, and Erin's father got up to leave. "I have to go tend the horses now."

"*You?*"

"Uh-huh. Mrs. Bromer's back really is worse. Mike did the work for her last night, and I'm on the schedule for this morning."

"*Mike* did?"

"Your brother is a perfectly nice person," said Mrs. Calahan sweetly. "Haven't you noticed?" She settled herself in the chair by the bedside. Don Calahan headed out the door.

"Dad," Erin called after him, "I'm sorry. I know I really messed up."

Her father stopped, turned around, and came back toward her. "Just get better soon," he said awkwardly.

"That's what I mean. The hospital bills—"

"The heck with the hospital bills!" Mr. Calahan's voice rose.

Tawnya Calahan hushed him with a glance. "Erin," she said after only a small pause, "the doctor is curious about those scratches on your arm."

"Huh?" Erin looked down at four red lines. "Oh. That must be where the bear turned me over."

Don Calahan stiffened and stared at her. "You mean, after the horse threw you—"

"She didn't throw me," said Erin with dignity, "I jumped."

Fifteen minutes later Erin's father finally left, shaking his head and muttering to himself, to feed and water horses for "the old hag."

Erin went home that same day. But she was not allowed out for a week, partly because she needed rest, and partly because she was, indeed, grounded, as her father told her rather gently at suppertime. In fact, there was no scolding of any kind, and only a few questions asked. Her parents seemed more concerned than angry, which made Erin feel very uneasy when she thought about it. Anger blew over, but concerned parents took action. . . .

The next day, as soon as she was allowed out of bed, she telephoned Aunt Lexie.

"Are you mad at me?" she asked, almost hopefully.

"More disappointed." The strong voice crackled in her ear. "What possessed you?"

"I felt like— I just had to get out and ride. The kids were picking on me. . . . "

In back of Erin, near the sink, Tawnya Calahan stood listening. She had taken time off from work to stay home with her daughter.

"Kids picking on you? What's that got to do with it? Let 'em pick." Aunt Lexie was not really scolding, either, Erin noted with a sinking heart, just lecturing. "You've got to *think* when you're around horses."

"Well, who'd ever think I'd meet up with a bear?"

"There's always something," Aunt Lexie said darkly. "Could have been anything. You could have cracked Spindrift's hooves on rocks, taking her out barefoot. Did you think of that?"

Erin held back a yelp. She had forgotten all about Spindrift's needing shoes. "No, I didn't," she admitted when she had got her breath back. "Is she all right?" she added anxiously.

"Cripes, girl, she's fine! Stop worrying."

"How about you? Your back—"

"Never mind my cussed back," Aunt Lexie fumed, and she hung up abruptly.

A get-well card from Aunt Lexie arrived the next day, a yellowed, flowery card with frosty sparkles on it. Once again Erin felt uneasy without quite knowing why. Aunt Lexie was not the card-sending sort—in fact, this one looked as if it had been in a box for years.

She squirmed under all the sympathy. There were

flowers from her grandparents in Arizona, and cards from other relatives and teachers, and even a few cards from kids. Though not, she was grateful to note, from Mikkie Orris.

She napped some of the time, read some of the time, did the schoolwork her teachers sent home for her, helped out with the housework but tried not to make a point of it. All the time she watched her parents like a small, cornered animal, waiting for their next move. But nothing happened. Toward the end of the week Mrs. Calahan went back to work, and still nothing had been said about whether Erin could keep Spindrift.

On Friday night she discovered the reason. It was because her parents had not yet managed to agree between themselves.

Lying awake very late at night, Erin heard them talking as they got ready for bed. At first their voices, not raised, were only a noise she dimly noticed. But then, when someone left a door open, she heard them plainly.

"It's the danger that bothers me," Don Calahan was saying.

"But there's always danger, whatever they do!"

Tawnya sounded frustrated. "Mike could get hurt playing ball. Either of them could get hit by a car, riding their bikes."

"I know, I know! But you didn't have to stand there and see her crumple up on the ground when she finally passed out."

"Don, you're too protective! You're going to have to let her grow up and take her lumps. The horse is helping, don't you see? She's taking risks, she's starting to speak out—maybe the wrong way, she's struggling, but you don't want to set her back now. You have to give her a chance. The horse has brought her out of herself. It's something she cares about."

"In one breath you tell me she's tough and she has to take her lumps, and in the next breath you tell me it would kill her if we took back the horse. And she's only had it less than two weeks!"

With an odd midnight calm Erin got up and opened her door. Instantly silence fell. Barefooted, in her pajamas, she padded to her parents' room and knocked on the door, which was hanging slightly ajar. After a small, surprised pause, her father came and pushed it all the way open.

"Can I come in?" Erin asked.

"Sure." But Don Calahan looked amazed.

Tawnya was already stretched out in the big double bed. Erin went and sat at her mother's feet.

"I heard you guys talking," she said, "and I didn't want to just lie there and eavesdrop."

"How come you're still awake?" her father asked her.

"Worrying about Spindrift. I know you want to get rid of her."

"But—we never said anything. . . . "

"I could tell. And there's all the hospital bills to pay, too, and if you sold Spindrift—"

"Good lord, forget the hospital bills, Erin! I mean, yes, there is a problem with money, and our insurance didn't cover everything. But we'll manage. Squirt, I never meant to upset you." Don Calahan was so upset himself that he started stammering under his daughter's sober gaze. "I—I—after what happened, I just thought—maybe you weren't ready."

"She wasn't," Tawnya Calahan said. "How could she be? But she's learning fast. Aren't you, Erin?"

Before Erin could answer, another voice broke in. "Can I come in, too?" Mike stood at the doorway, yawning.

"This doesn't concern you," his mother told him.

"It sort of does. Family business. If I keep my mouth shut?"

Don Calahan motioned him in with a what-the-heck gesture. "The more, the merrier. Now, Squirt, you were saying?"

"I was saying," Erin answered slowly, "that I know I did something really stupid." She said it in Aunt Lexie's matter-of-fact way, not just to tell her parents what they wanted to hear, but because it was true. Days of thinking had shown her part of what growing up meant. She said, "It'll be my own fault if you decide to sell Spindrift. And, if you let me keep her, I know I'll have to prove to you that I'm ready now."

Mr. Calahan's gaze shifted to his wife, then back to his daughter. "Yes?" he prompted.

Erin tried to explain. "There's lots of things about having a horse I never knew. I mean, I thought it would be all just, like, riding. But I have to think about, you know, family, because you guys are the ones paying for her. And I have to think about the horse and all the things she needs, because she's mine, and I have to take care of her. And I have to think about me, too, and sometimes I have to make

Spindrift do things she doesn't like, and— Well, that day I went riding by myself, I just wasn't thinking or I would have at least left a note. But now I know I've got to think."

Don Calahan looked at his wife again. "Tawn, you're right," he said in wonder. "There has been a change."

"I know I can do better now," Erin said. "I mean, it's been knocked into my head." She swallowed, and asked the question that had been haunting her. "May I keep Spindrift?"

"I think you deserve another chance," Tawnya answered gently.

"Yes, Squirt. I feel better about it now. Just, please, no more escapades. All right?" Her father was beaming at her. Erin got up and hugged him.

"Okay. But, Dad—" She was too tired to show him all her relief, and also too tired to be angry. Just weary enough to blurt something out. "I hate it when you call me Squirt."

"What?" He could not believe what he was hearing.

"I hate it when you call me Squirt," she repeated, clearly and without raising her voice.

"But—but, Erin, it's your pet name! To show

you I love you. I don't mean any harm by it." Don Calahan felt hurt, and Erin could hear it in his voice. She sank back to her seat on the bed, shoulders rounded. Everything had been beautiful until she had opened her mouth. . . .

"That's right, Dad," Mike spoke up suddenly. "Lay a load of guilt on her."

"Michael!" His mother was outraged.

But Don Calahan said, "No, he's right. I'm way out of line. When somebody speaks up and tells me an honest thing, I should listen." He touched Erin lightly on the shoulder. "Come on, Sq— Erin, I mean. Get to bed." He made sweeping gestures. "Mike, you too! Everybody out!"

"Good night, little sister," Mike told her nastily in the hallway. Erin smiled at him, a warm, wide smile. Hard for Mike to be too nice for too long. And it was, indeed, a good night.

The next day, Saturday, Erin spent some time pacing around in her room like a thoroughbred in a too-small stall. Finally, sighing, she sat down at her desk. Much as she wanted always to ride, ride, ride, every day, all summer, she knew now that her horse was not something she could take for granted. Her parents worked hard to make the money that paid the board. It would be only fair if she spent some of her time helping.

She got out some scraps of poster paper, cut them into small rectangles, and began to letter her business cards: Erin Calahan. Babysitting. And her phone number.

Also on Saturday, one last special get-well card arrived, a handmade one, from Marcy Gilmore.

"A friend of yours brought this by," Tawnya told Erin, handing it to her, "but I thought you were asleep, and I didn't want to wake you."

Friend? What friend? She had never run around with the other kids much, and even less since she had gotten Spindrift. She had been too busy with her horse.

She understood when she took the stiff white art-paper card out of its oversized envelope. There was Marcy's best-effort pencil drawing of Spindrift, carefully tinted with watercolor. Inside was another drawing, this one of the mare's head. "She's worth it," the message read. "Get well soon. Love, Marcy."

Chapter Eight

"Grumpy as ever, I see," Erin complained, standing at the stall door and looking in at Spindrift. She did not really mind the mare's sulkiness, happy as she was to be back. She was just teasing. "Here I am, haven't been to see you for a whole week, and all you can do is show me your hind end."

Spindrift stood at the far corner of her stall with her back turned, refusing to come to the halter. Only the slight movements of her ears showed that she heard Erin at all. Aunt Lexie, moving stiffly, came to look. The old woman was wearing a brace for her back, and she acted nearly as grouchy as the mare.

"That's just the way she is," she snapped.

"Just like some people are old hags?" Erin gave Aunt Lexie a daring, playful look. In a giddy mood, she was not letting anyone's grumpiness touch her. Aunt Lexie stared, then barked out a short laugh.

"That's right. She's a good, steady horse, but she just has to have her say. Look at her now."

Spindrift had swung her head around to glare at them over her shoulder. Erin laughed.

"Some people are just born difficult," said Aunt Lexie more softly.

"Come on, girl." Erin showed the mare a jelly bean, holding it out on her open palm. Very, very slowly, one short step at a time, Spindrift came to get it. Erin haltered the horse, then gave her a crushing hug around her neck and a big, mushy kiss on her soft nose. Spindrift stiffened and rolled her eyes in shock.

"She's outraged," said Aunt Lexie, amused. "Her dignity's hurt."

"Difficult people need love like everybody else," Erin told the mare. She led Spindrift out of her stall and cross-tied her, then began to groom her, humming a tune to herself.

"She's been enjoying her vacation," Aunt Lexie added after a while. "She knows you work her—that's why she's acting so sour. You riding today?"

Erin stopped humming, and a small frown made a line between her eyebrows. "No, I guess not today," she said. "I'll just walk her."

"Oh." Aunt Lexie was surprised, and let it show. "I thought the doctor gave you a clean bill of health."

"I'm feeling okay. But my hunt cap is smashed. I don't have a new one yet."

"Your brother said you were going to use his old bicycling helmet."

"Oh. Well, I—I don't know where it is."

"It's right in the tack room, hanging by your bridle."

"Oh." Erin fussed with Spindrift's forelock, arranging it first over one eye, then over the other. "I'm just going to walk her today, anyway."

Aunt Lexie stared hard at her. "Young lady," she said flatly, "you are scared."

"I am not!" yelled Erin.

"And no wonder," Aunt Lexie added, as if she

were just talking to herself. "I know how that goes. No time to be scared while it's happening, so you think about it afterward. Bad fall. You were hurt. But when I remember the girl who came out here and just couldn't wait to ride . . ."

"You *are* an old hag!" Erin shouted at her.

"Listen, kiddo." Aunt Lexie came closer, peering at her, an odd, focused look on her face. "I've got opinions on this. I fell, and I'd give anything to be able to get on a horse and ride again. You fell, and you *can*."

"I will!" Erin yelled. "Tomorrow!"

"Seems to me," said Aunt Lexie, "that it'll get harder the longer you wait."

Erin stood feeling miserable. If bad dreams meant scared, then that was what she was, all right—scared. Dreams of the tree branches waving crazily, and the sick, helpless feeling of being flung through the air and falling, falling, and the growl of the bear. Sometimes the dream started as soon as she closed her eyes to go to sleep. If it was just a matter of being afraid it would be all right—she could walk away. But she loved Spindrift.

"I was so scared Dad was going to take her back,"

she told Aunt Lexie in a low voice, "I didn't have time to be scared about—about the other thing until the last couple of nights."

"He really was that upset? I thought so." Aunt Lexie nodded with sympathy. "Daddies and their little girls. Almost as hard for them to learn as it is for the kids. That all straightened out now?"

"I think."

"Are you worried that if you ride and fall, maybe he'll want to sell Spindrift again?"

Erin shook her head. "No. No, my dad's okay, and Mom's on my side. No, I'm just scared." She swallowed. "What if she does it again?"

"Rears under you, you mean?" Aunt Lexie sounded very gentle, for an old hag. "Why would she? You planning to go find yourself another bear?"

It could happen again—Erin knew it could. Though it wasn't likely. . . . Nothing was ever simple.

"You survived," Aunt Lexie added.

"I'm just walking her today, anyway," Erin said in a small voice.

Aunt Lexie looked at her, then suddenly gave in. "Okay. No rush. You want me to show you how to longe her?"

Even longeing was not as simple as it looked, she

learned. A small change in the angle of the leading arm would make Spindrift balk, and a careless movement of the whip would make her bolt. Spindrift did not know how to act on the longe line. "I thought as much," Aunt Lexie grumbled. Patiently she showed the mare what she wanted, again and again. At first Spindrift would cut in toward the center of the circle, leaving a loop of line dangling. Warned away with the whip, she would lash out with her heels. Longeing could be dangerous. But Spindrift learned quickly.

"Here," said Aunt Lexie at last, turning the line over to Erin. "Just, whatever you do, don't get tangled in the slack."

Don't put your finger through a halter ring. Don't get caught in a loop of lead rope or rein. The horse is strong enough to hurt you without even knowing. Rules tenteen, eleventeen, and twelvety.

"Get behind her, drive her," Aunt Lexie ordered. "Look at her butt, not her head!"

Spindrift had balked, trying to turn back the wrong way. Erin went to her head, careful to gather up the longe line, and got her going clockwise again.

"That's her bad side," said Aunt Lexie. "Keep her moving. She needs more work on that side."

"Huh?"

"Horses are right-handed or left-handed, just like people. That's her bad side. She's stiff on that side—she needs to learn to bend that way. Keep her going twice as long that way when you longe her."

Silence for several minutes, as Erin concentrated on working her horse. Spindrift began to glisten with a light sweat.

"Switch the chain and let her walk the other way to cool off," Aunt Lexie said. "Who's that watching from up by the road?"

Erin looked and did not answer. She wasn't sure in the late-afternoon light, but she thought it looked like Marcy Gilmore.

Back in school the next morning, Erin found that her accident had made her something of a celebrity. The kids wanted to see her claw scratches, and were disappointed when she told them they were already gone. For that matter, so was the bear. It had been captured by the Forest Service, taken away, and released in a state park a hundred miles distant.

"But I won't be able to ride down there anymore," Erin told Marcy, "not unless I can find someone to come with me. Spindrift will remember." She frowned, wondering when she would find the courage to ride at all, and Marcy looked at her oddly, saying nothing.

That afternoon Aunt Lexie was puttering around the stable in her oldest pair of polyester slacks, a torn scarf on her head, hefting electric clippers. She had some colts and fillies to tend to.

"Buyers coming next week," she explained crisply. "Got to get them looking decent. You riding?"

"I'll just walk her around," Erin said.

"Okay."

Erin took Spindrift on the lead line, up along the road, then down behind the development along the woods. The mare was behaving beautifully, not even thinking about charging ahead. . . .

A dog ran out of a clump of blackberry bushes, and the next thing Erin knew there was a great and startling explosion of energy beside her, like a pheasant bursting into flight only far larger, and the nylon lead was snapping through her hands. By themselves, so it seemed, the hands tightened on the knot at the end of the lead and tugged, tightening the chain, bringing the mare down. Erin stood, with the skin of her palms burning, staring at Spindrift. No use scolding a scared horse—it would just scare her more. The dog was gone, and the mare seemed calm again. Taking a deep breath, Erin turned and walked on, inwardly quaking.

"She shied," Erin reported to Aunt Lexie.

"They'll do that," Aunt Lexie grunted, not even looking up from the fetlock she was trimming.

The next day Spindrift shied at the loud whistle of a bird as Erin led her out to the longe ring. The day after that, being walked again, she sprang back with a snort from a crumpled potato-chip bag caught in the roadside weeds. Erin gave a tug on the chain and sighed. She had to admit, the potato-chip bag had moved in the breeze. Still, she had not expected owning a horse to be like this, always something to tend to, problems to be dealt with, fears to be faced. . . . She walked on.

A few minutes later Spindrift shied at, of all things, a mailbox. "Silly girl," Erin told her, not at all impressed.

Back at the barn, she groomed her horse for hours, clipping her whiskers and fetlocks, putting a braid in her mane, just for fun. "So *pretty*," she told the mare when she was finished.

Spindrift paid no attention to the sweet talk or to any amount of patting or fussing. She never did.

"Stuck-up wossie."

The horse's indifference did not bother Erin anymore. Sometime over the last few days the mare had come into clear focus for her. Not a bigger-than-life dream horse any longer, but her very own Spindrift, the grouch. Spindrift the iron-bellied, who would eat anything. Spindrift, who liked jelly beans best. Spindrift, who had to be herself. A real horse. Hardly scary at all—from the ground.

She had not mentioned at home that she was not riding, and her parents, assuming that she was, had not found out. "How's the horse?" they would ask at dinnertime each day, and Erin would answer, "Fine."

But somehow Mike knew.

He had an instinct for these things, Erin thought afterward, remembering how she had learned to ride a bike.

Or perhaps he was in cahoots with Aunt Lexie. Because when Erin walked into the stable on Saturday morning, Aunt Lexie was not there. But Mike stood, big as life, talking to Spindrift through the stall bars. Erin goggled at her brother.

"I thought you had a game or something."

" 'Or something,' " he mimicked. "Is that the way you follow my athletic career? Let me see you get this wild mustang out of the stall."

Erin bribed and coaxed Spindrift over to be haltered, all the time with her mind on Mike. What was he doing in her hideaway? Of course, he had fed and watered for Aunt Lexie the whole time Erin had been laid up, so he knew his way around the stable. Still, she had never expected to see him there.

"Hey, really," she said, "aren't you missing practice?"

"Do you really care?" Mike grinned at her in open challenge. "I'm not leaving until I see you ride this fierce wossie."

"I'll ride her when I'm good and ready!" Erin flared.

"Ready, my eye. You're scared."

"I am not!"

"Don't give me that. You haven't been on her since the day she threw you."

"So? It's no business of yours."

They argued while Erin groomed Spindrift. Mike lounged against a stall in an irritating way, elbows up, as if he was prepared to stay all day. Erin took her time picking hooves, combing mane and tail. Mike was not fooled.

"Where's that saddle?" he demanded. "Do I have to go get it myself?"

"I am not riding today," Erin shouted, "just because you say so!"

"Oh, yes you are, little sister!" With a sudden spurt of energy Mike straightened, strode to the tack room, and came out with his old bicycling helmet. As Erin stared he plopped it on her head and adjusted the chin strap to fit her.

"Saddle," he ordered.

"I am *not*—" Erin started, nearly in tears. Then she stopped what she had been going to say. Mike was not going to give in like Aunt Lexie, she knew. If the world were ending in fifteen minutes—and she felt as if it might—Mike would be pestering her just the same. Even as she thought it, he grinned.

"Chicken," he crooned, as if they were both little kids. "Chicken! Dare ya!"

She glared at him and went to get the gear. Not even a chance of rain; there was not a cloud in the sky. . . . She was going to have to do it.

Aunt Lexie happened to be walking down the driveway as Erin led her mare out.

"That's my girl!" she said warmly. "Just take her in the ring, Erin. You know she's not going to do anything in there."

Aunt Lexie had planned this with Mike; Erin felt sure of it. "You two make me sick," she said, taking Spindrift through the gate. Not answering, Aunt Lexie and Mike folded their arms atop the fence, watching.

Erin sighed, snapped the stirrups down the leathers, gathered her reins, and mounted. She sat for a long moment finding her foot position, letting her heels drop, finding her proper balance in the saddle. Looking down at ground that seemed much too far below.

Deep breath. . . .

She squeezed with her legs. Spindrift started into an easy walk.

And as soon as the mare was moving between her knees, Erin felt a familiar, forgotten surge of joy, and the world spread itself at her feet once again. The wide world, hers for riding in. And no matter how she tried to prevent it, a broad, happy grin crept onto her face.

"Still mad at us?" Aunt Lexie called, smiling.

"Run her!" Mike yelled.

She would have loved to. But though Spindrift could have cantered down a country lane with her, she was not yet well enough balanced to manage the curves of the ring without stumbling. Erin trotted her instead, and varied the pace from jog to extended trot back to walk again.

"First-rate, kiddo," Aunt Lexie told her afterward, after Mike had gone to the ball field, while Erin was cooling Spindrift and brushing her dry.

"I don't know why I waited so long," Erin admitted.

Aunt Lexie shrugged. "You're young, you're learning. Now you've found out. When rotten things happen, you just have to keep going, Erin. Believe me, I know."

Chapter Nine

"When the farrier comes to shoe her," Erin told Marcy happily, "I can ride her out!"

"The vet come yet?"

"While I was laid up. She stood real still for her shots, Aunt Lexie said."

Nearly every school day Marcy sat with Erin on the bus either in the morning or in the afternoon, and she always wanted to hear news of Spindrift. Unlike her parents, Erin thought, who seemed to ask about her horse just to ask, Marcy was really interested. She, too, had read every horse book in the school library three times.

"I can't wait to canter her. She's getting more collected on the longe. She used to go along all strung out."

"Will you ride her at the canter on the trail?"

"Sure!"

"Where will you ride?"

"Back by the woods. Anywhere except where the bear was." Erin sighed. Her rides would still be short for a while, the countryside beyond those far woods still beckoning, calling to her. "Aunt Lexie says the best way to get her through there would be to pony her, go with somebody else on horseback. Horses always act braver when they're with each other."

"Wish I could come," Marcy murmured.

"Dipstick," Mikkie Orris suddenly accused from across the aisle. "How's the horse, Dipstick?"

Feeling good, Erin just smiled at her. Lucky as she was, she couldn't blame Mikkie too much for calling her names. After all, she had a horse, and Mikkie didn't.

Springtime days, each one a little longer than the last. Erin was dreaming of summer days, when she would be able to spend hour upon hour with her beloved horse. She worked Spindrift at walk and trot in the training ring, feeling the mare respond more willingly to her touch on the reins, to her signals with the leg. Twenty minutes of longeing three times a week, plus Aunt Lexie's careful feeding, had already reduced the hay belly. Erin knew it when she was able to start using a shorter girth, a good leather one, instead of the cotton-cord one in its fuzzy cover. And Spindrift's shoulders and hindquarters were already showing some muscle, and her neck was beginning to arch.

The farrier came to shoe Spindrift Thursday evening. Erin watched in awe as he rasped her hooves level, measured their angle with his gauge, fitted and nailed on the shoes. The farrier said Spindrift was a nice horse. He probably said that to nearly everyone, but Erin felt proud.

Friday after school, then, was the time for her to ride Spindrift out.

It rained in the morning, to Erin's mixed dismay and relief—she was still a little bit afraid. But it cleared by afternoon, and she discovered that she very much wanted to ride. She ran home from the bus stop and rushed through her chores, but made sure she did them all—these days she always made sure she emptied the dishwasher and set the table. At the stable, Aunt Lexie was waiting.

"You know you're likely to have some trouble with her," the old woman warned. "She'll remember the last time you rode her out. She's had plenty of time to think about it."

Erin shrugged. Best to meet trouble head-on. She planned not ever to let fear get the better of her again. She sweet-talked Spindrift out of her stall, patted her, then groomed and tacked her up in silence. In a short time she led her out and mounted as Aunt Lexie stood at the mare's head.

"Keep her to the walk when you go out alone, for now," said Aunt Lexie, looking worried. "You have your headgear?"

Erin just nodded, although the bicycling helmet was right on top of her head for anyone to see.

"Safety bars open?"

Erin nodded again. They always were.

"Don't go anywhere except where you told me."

"I *know*," said Erin, losing patience.

Aunt Lexie stepped back with a sigh. "I wish I

could go with you," she said. "It would be so much easier. But my confounded back . . . Well, be careful."

"Off we go, girl!" Erin signaled for the walk. Spindrift lifted her head and planted her feet, swaying backward.

"Leg!" Aunt Lexie shouted, and Erin kicked. Spindrift started off, but slowly, weaving from side to side of the lane.

"What did she do that for?" Erin called. But Aunt Lexie was out of earshot.

"Are you sick?" she asked her horse. The mare's ears were tilted at an odd angle, as if she was listening back over her shoulders, and there seemed to be a catch in her walk as they reached the end of the lane. . . .

Without any reason or warning that Erin could see, Spindrift shied hard, spun around, and started back for the barn at a headlong gallop. Erin was flung up over her neck, standing in the stirrups. She grabbed hold of the mane to stay on. "Whoa!" she shouted, pulling back hard on both reins with her one free hand. But Spindrift, if anything, ran faster. Still jerking at the reins, Erin tried to settle her weight in the saddle, but she was jounced about crazily. The mare was paying no attention to her at all. Fence posts whirled by at a dizzying speed. Aside from sheer terror, Erin felt all the angry shame of being run away with, and another rule, perhaps number millihundred, flashed through her mind: Never let your horse canter back to the barn. Though what Spindrift was doing could hardly be called a canter.

"Aunt Lexie," Erin yelled, "look out!"

The mare was trying to run right into the stable, right into her stall! Erin ducked, lying low on the horse's neck. But Aunt Lexie was ready for her, and closed the big door with a rumble. Spindrift slid to a lurching stop as it banged shut—if Erin had not been lying on her neck already, she would have been over it and off, for sure. The mare sidled right up to the stable wall, pressing Erin's leg against the brick. Erin kicked angrily, with no result, as Aunt Lexie stood with her knuckles on her hips.

"Well," said Aunt Lexie, "you didn't go where you told me after all."

"What is the *matter* with this horse?" Erin cried. "She ran away with me!"

"Barn sour." Aunt Lexie came up and took hold of the bridle by the cheek strap. "I told you you'd have trouble. Think she has her monthlies, too. That makes them touchy, mares. Just like us. You all right?"

Erin scarcely heard. "How could she *do* that to me!" she wailed.

"She didn't do it to you," Aunt Lexie said. "Nothing personal. She just did it, and you happened to be on her at the time."

Erin stared. "Sheesh," she said more calmly. "It's like my dad said. One thing after another."

Aunt Lexie smiled. "Yup," she agreed. "You stayed with her very well," she added. "Now listen, in case that happens again . . ."

She was to pull the horse's head around, making her circle. Or jiggle the bit, two-handed, rocking it from side to side, since a horse tends to lean against a bit that is pulled straight back. Or pulley rein—strictly an emergency measure, as it hurts the horse. Even angry and frightened as she was, her heart still pounding, Erin wondered if she could ever hurt Spindrift.

"Now," said Aunt Lexie, her tone growing stern, "you take her in the training ring and work the buns off her. An hour, two hours, until she figures it's not worth her while to run back to the barn."

Erin signaled the horse to walk. Spindrift pinned her ears back and stood where she was, by the stable, looking like a small white mule. Chewing her pipe, Aunt Lexie strode into the tack room, coming out a moment later with a riding crop.

"You know how to use a stick? Behind the saddle, no harder than you have to, but hard enough to make her do what you say. Now ride her into that ring."

It took ten minutes. Spindrift moved once the crop was in Erin's hand—she had seen it. But she scooted backward, danced sideways, balked and spun in her efforts to stay by the barn. Once forced near the ring, she refused the gate until Erin sent her through with a hard kick, a lick, and a yell. Erin had never fought with a horse before, and the whole process was against her way of thinking that the horse should be her friend, friend, friend—but anger helped her. Blast Spindrift, anyway, the stupid, stuck-up, grouchy mare, she would show her. She owned her, and she would ride her, and phooey on her. Aunt Lexie closed the gate behind the mare's flying tail, then stayed by it to coach.

"Trot her out! Eight, ten times around. Keep her going when she wants to stop."

Erin trotted her, posting until her legs ached. Fully

roused, Spindrift kept trying to break into a gallop. The training ring slowed her, and Erin would bring her back with a rocking bit, make her go in circles until she was dizzy.

"That's it. . . . Go the other way now."

Erin was sweating nearly as hard as the horse. She brought a hand up to wipe her forehead, glanced at Aunt Lexie, then peered. Someone was standing beside the old woman, someone young—Marcy? No. Hi yi yi, it was Mike.

Spindrift took advantage of the moment's break in her concentration to dart toward the barn.

"Circle!" Aunt Lexie yelled.

"Check it out," said Mike in an awed tone. "That Spindrift is spinning for sure."

"*And* drifting toward the barn," Alexandra Bromer snapped. "Erin! Straighten her out! Kick her up toward the other end."

Spindrift lifted her forelegs in a low rear.

"Hands low! Stay with her! Crop! Leg!"

"I don't believe it," Mike breathed. "She can really ride!"

"That she can," said Mrs. Bromer curtly. "She has a good seat and first-rate hands. All she needs is some experience. Erin! Make her do figure eights!"

They watched awhile longer as Erin struggled with the mare.

"That's it!" Mrs. Bromer hollered at Erin after a while. "Keep her busy. Turn her around. Now back her up. Okay, do some serpentines. After that, diagonals. Whatever it takes to get her listening to you."

The serpentines were ragged, the diagonals bent toward the barn. But within an hour Spindrift was walking quietly around the training ring and yielding on the bit.

"Show's over for today," said Aunt Lexie to Mike. "Tell your mother that Erin will be late, please. That mare is going to take a lot of cooling."

"Check it out!" Mike murmured as he left. "Awesome."

Erin arrived home very late and smelling strongly of sweat and horse. She had to shower before she ate. Her father had cooked his specialty, chicken tetrazzini, and her mother was stirring stewed tomatoes. They'd waited for her without much complaining.

"I couldn't believe it," Mike told the family over supper. "Erin really looked like she knew what she was doing."

Erin glanced at her brother with a frown, waiting for the other shoe to drop. So did her parents. It was not like Mike to be openly nice. He took their stares as expressions of doubt.

"I really mean it! She looked super. And the horse was rearing and bucking and cutting the cheese and everything."

"Mike!" said Tawnya Calahan, shocked.

"Spindrift was *not* bucking," Erin said hotly.

Mr. Calahan had his eyebrows raised high. "She was misbehaving?"

"Aunt Lexie says it's about time she tested me out. She says I won. It probably won't happen again, or not so bad."

Aunt Lexie had also said something about working Spindrift at the canter within the next week. Erin smiled, then sighed. Spindrift's headlong gallop had certainly been a new, bone-jarring experience compared to William's floating carousel-horse gait. She wondered how long Aunt Lexie had worked with William on his canter.

"She wasn't even hanging on!" Mike exclaimed. "How can you stay on without hanging on?"

"Balance." She still could not believe he really meant what he was saying.

"Aren't you afraid you'll fall off?"

"I fell off William lots of times, learning to ride."
The hunt cap and the soft dirt of the ring had always
taken the worst of it. "There's nothing to it. So why
hang on?"

Mr. Calahan stared hard at her. "You never told
me that!"

"Well, anyway, she looked *mean*," said Mike. "The
Squirt can really ride."

"Stop calling me Squirt," Erin told him calmly,
almost relieved that he was being nasty at last. She
knew he just did it to make her mad. "There's a lot
of things I never told you," she said to her father.

His eyebrows shot up. "Such as?"

"Such as—" She took a huge bite of tetrazzini and
chewed it thoroughly, enjoying his silent impatience, her mother's curious look. And neither of
them could order her to talk with her mouth full,
after all the times they had ordered her not to.

"Such as," she said finally, swallowing, "if you
get any phone calls for a babysitter, it's because I
went around the development and told people I would.
Time I earned some money to help pay for horse
bills."

"You what?" Don Calahan exclaimed.

"Went around the development. Door to door. With a bunch of cards I made, sort of like business cards, with my name and phone number on them."

"You did that?" Tawnya Calahan sounded as surprised as her husband. "When?"

Erin shrugged. "Different days. Whenever it rained too hard to ride in. And people were real nice. I offered to walk dogs, too."

"I'll be darned," said Don Calahan. "That was really spunky, Sq— Erin."

"But do you know how to babysit?" added her mother anxiously.

"I'll learn," said Erin. "You know I learn real fast." She grinned at her mother. "And I hope they ask me mostly at night. When I can't ride anyway."

Chapter Ten

Aunt Lexie told Erin to work Spindrift on the ground, with a lead chain, reviewing "whoa" and "back." Erin kept at it until the mare obeyed without pulling against the chain. Then she would reward her with a jelly bean. After a few days of this, it was time for Erin to ride Spindrift again. Aunt Lexie sucked at her pipe for a while, then put a different bit on the bridle, a bit with a jointed mouthpiece like a snaffle but short shanks like a curb.

"Called a Tom Thumb," she explained briefly. "Little more severe. Make her pay attention, but keep your hands light unless she gives you trouble."

Erin nodded.

"She's been out all night," Aunt Lexie said, "and I longed her this morning, so she's tired. She should behave. But don't figure on going far."

She gave Erin instructions. Ride halfway down the lane, then turn back. Spindrift would probably balk when walking away from the barn and try to rush coming back. Erin was to push her past the barn and take her up the driveway, to the road, and then back.

"Do that maybe fifteen, twenty times. Keep pushing her past the barn until she doesn't know whether she's coming or going. Take her around the house and back, into the ring and back, wherever else you can think of. Keep her guessing. Maybe one time go all the way down to the woods, and another time just as far as the house. And keep at it until she gives up on the barn. Fake her out. The more she doesn't know what's going on, the more she has to listen to you. You got it?"

Erin nodded and swung herself into the saddle. "Whoa!" she ordered fiercely as she put her weight in the stirrup, and Spindrift stood perfectly still for her.

"She learns," Aunt Lexie said, lifting her pipe in a sort of salute. "She learns fast. All she needs is to be worked with. Now, who's this coming?"

A gleaming Mercedes was pulling into the driveway. Aunt Lexie shaded her eyes, peering. "Must be the buyers," she muttered.

"Should I go home?" asked Erin.

"Heck, no. That Spindrift's a credit to any stable, even as sourpussy as she is. Go ahead and take her out. Make her whoa and back up if she gets too bullheaded."

Erin did. It was a good two hours before the mare stopped swerving toward the stable at every pass. During that time Erin saw Aunt Lexie showing a well-dressed woman and man six yearling colts and fillies and four two-year-olds, putting them through their paces on halter and longe and driving reins. Aunt Lexie looked out of place beside her visitors in her muddy duck boots and her old army-surplus jacket. It shouldn't matter, Erin thought. The colts were beautiful.

When the buyers were gone and Spindrift was put away, Erin went out and found Aunt Lexie leaning against the pasture fence. Slumped, rather.

"I don't understand it," Aunt Lexie said aloud, talking to the air. "Anybody with sense knows a Morgan is supposed to be a tough all-purpose horse. But these days all they think about is the show ring. Grow their hooves long, put chains on their feet, make 'em step high. Keep 'em in stalls all the time, good for nothing but showing. They're raising them oversize and long-legged, willowy, no substance. Sissy looking."

"Didn't they buy any?" Erin asked.

"Oh, yes, they bought some. And there's others that come, and they buy, too. Some. But never enough, and never at a fair price. 'Old style,' they call my colts. Ever since my old stallion died a few years back, I've been losing money. Heck, by the time I pay the stud fee and the feed bill and the vetting and what not, it's not worth it." Aunt Lexie sighed. "I tell you, kiddo, I'm going to have to give it up."

Erin listened silently, not alarmed. Adults often talked in this gloomy manner, she had found.

"Mares don't take, half the time, anyway," Aunt Lexie burst out. "What with trailering to the stud, and foal heat, and having to take the foal along. It's just too iffy to get them bred right, and I hate to trailer a foal to the stud. Half my mares, at any time, I'm feeding them and they aren't producing. It doesn't pay."

"Why don't you get your own stud again?" Erin asked. "I'd like to see a mare get bred sometime."

"Because I'm in no shape to handle a stallion anymore." Aunt Lexie straightened, making a face. "Ooooh, my back. I overdid it."

"I'll water and feed," said Erin, and Aunt Lexie gave her a crooked smile.

"It's a good thing I have you around, kiddo."

Within the next few days Erin started riding Spindrift down along the woods again. All went well and the rides were lovely, great clumps of phlox and crowsfoot in bloom along the trails. Within a few days, also, she began to canter her mare in the small, circular ring. The size of it, just large enough for longeing, kept Spindrift at a slow, easy canter. Those first few canters were awkward, but Erin no longer expected things to be perfect right away. After some practice, she and her mare would move into the larger ring. And then—the end of school just a few weeks away, and the whole summer before her, the world at her feet . . .

The middle of the week brought beautiful May weather. Thursday afternoon Erin started off on Spindrift, trail riding. With a wave to Aunt Lexie, she took her mare at a nice jog down the lane. Everything seemed, at last, to be going right. Only a few days more of school, she was already making some money babysitting, and she was back on her horse, where she loved to be, in the warm, warm May sunshine. . . . The broodmares stood lazily in it, swishing flies. The foals were sunning themselves. Old William seemed to be enjoying it, too, stretched out flat on his side in the middle of his paddock—

Erin looked again, then halted Spindrift and stared. Flies had settled all over William, and he was making no effort to shake them off. And shouldn't she be able to see his ribs moving when he breathed?

Erin spun her mare and sent her at a canter back up the lane, as she was not supposed to do. Aunt Lexie came hurrying out, looking annoyed, and Erin brought Spindrift to a hasty halt in front of her.

"What the devil—"

"Aunt Lexie," Erin interrupted, her voice shaking, "William is down, and there are flies on him, and I don't see him moving."

Alexandra Bromer stared. Then, arms flung wide

for balance, her stocky body jouncing painfully, she started at a stubborn, limping run down the lane.

Erin sat on Spindrift and watched her go. The mare was dancing, excited by her brief run, and Erin patted her and talked to her softly to settle her. When Spindrift was calm, Erin sent her at a slow walk down the lane. She did not want to come to the paddock before Aunt Lexie did.

She got there at last, tied Spindrift's reins to a fence post—another thing she was not supposed to do—and went in, although she did not really want to. The gate was hanging wide open. Aunt Lexie was kneeling in the grass by William, chasing the flies off him with fiercely swinging arms. As Erin watched, Aunt Lexie gave up on the flies, slumped sideways, so that she sat in the grass, and heaved William's heavy, lifeless head into her lap.

"Poor baby," she said in tight, angry tones. "Poor William." She did not look at Erin, but sat stroking the horse's bony forehead. "His old heart must have stopped, just like that, and he was all alone, no one to be with him, and I hope it was quick. . . . I guess it was quick. I don't see any grass torn up or anything like that. Do you?" She glanced up at Erin, a quick, hard glance, and Erin was startled to see that her old eyes were glittering with tears. She shook her head, and Aunt Lexie laid William's head down off her lap and struggled up.

"Got to call the rendering plant, I suppose. . . . Where's my pipe?" Aunt Lexie fumbled in the breast pocket of her plaid hunting shirt, found the pipe, and looked at it as if she did not know what it was. "Drat it!" she exploded. Turning, she flung the pipe away over her shoulder and strode up the hill toward the house. Erin untied Spindrift's reins and followed her, leading the mare.

Limping and puffing, Aunt Lexie soon slowed her pace. "Aren't you going out riding now, after all?" she asked Erin.

"No . . . I guess not."

"Well. I have to admit I'm glad you're here, kid."

Abruptly she stopped walking and leaned against the nearest fence post, leaned heavily, staring down toward the woods.

"Don't have anyone else who gives a crap about me. Got that horse when Mr. Bromer left me—"

"Mr. Bromer?" Erin blurted, surprised. Though she knew Aunt Lexie was called Mrs. Bromer, it had never occurred to her that there was a Mr. Bromer.

"Yup. Rotten bum. Gave up my horses for a horse's behind when I married him." Aunt Lexie's tone was as bitter as iodine, harsh as a farrier's rasp. "Haven't heard a word from him for twenty years. When he left, first thing I did I went out and bought myself a horse, and it was William. . . ."

The name trailed away into a gulp. Aunt Lexie plunged off into a hard walk toward the house again, and Erin, not knowing what else to do, hurried along beside her in silence until they reached the stable. Then she took Spindrift in, untacked her, and groomed her for a long time, feeling the touch of the future like the tap of a cold finger on her shoulder. Someday Spindrift would die. . . . She sighed and rested her face against Spindrift's neck, and the mare stood still for her.

Aunt Lexie had gone into her house and did not come out. Erin took care of the evening feeding, as she often did, and went home.

Her mother and father were there in the kitchen. "William died," said Erin.

"Aunt Lexie's old horse?" It was Mrs. Calahan.

"He was just lying in the paddock, dead."

Tawnya Calahan heard something extra in Erin's

voice, and looked up from the apples she was peeling. Don Calahan heard it, too, and turned around where he stood by the stove.

"She threw her pipe away. Said she's got nobody who cares about her. She's had William for twenty years."

Don and Tawnya Calahan glanced at each other. Then Mrs. Calahan went over to the wall telephone and started to dial. "We're having her over for supper."

"Do you think the old hag, or old bag, will come?" asked Mr. Calahan. Aunt Lexie's self-chosen title had become something of a joke in the family since the night of the bear crisis.

"Maybe, if I twist her arm. . . . Hello, Mrs. Bromer? This is Tawnya Calahan. Erin told us about William, and we're very sorry. . . ."

Aunt Lexie's voice was not as sharp as usual, but somewhat muffled. Erin could not hear what she said.

"Yes. Well, listen, we want you to come over for dinner." Mrs. Calahan used her most positive tone. "No use sitting there by yourself. We're having roast pork, and there's plenty—"

"Cripes!" Aunt Lexie's voice had gotten back some

of its usual power. "So that's what I have to do to get invited to dinner. Have a dead horse."

"Well, we didn't know you all that well. . . ." Tawnya Calahan was so taken aback that she started laughing. "We'll have to make sure to invite you soon on some happier occasion. But come tonight, for a start. Shall I send Don for you?"

"Heck, no. I can find my own way. You want me to bring some wine?"

"If you like. I'm not sure what goes with pork and sauerkraut."

"I'll find something," said Aunt Lexie grimly, and she hung up.

"There," said Tawnya Calahan in uncertain tones. "That wasn't so bad."

Don Calahan looked at her. "So how come you're shaking?"

The dinner was much more cheerful than anyone might have expected. Aunt Lexie came in her best red polyester slacks and a startling top with sequins and glitter, maybe left over from somebody's Christmas party. And a blaze of red lipstick, a red badge of courage worn proudly. I am not going to let it get me down, Aunt Lexie's lipstick said, and the dinner took its tone from her: good times in the midst of bad. No sniffling, no tiptoeing around.

"So how's the old bag?" asked Don Calahan as he seated her.

"Fair," she shot back.

"Good. Ahem." He cleared his throat. "So this is the William H. Bromer memorial dinner, I understand."

"H?"

"Horse," he told her meekly, and she laughed.

She praised William, the real mashed potatoes, and the hot baked apples with cinnamon and nutmeg and butter. By dessert time the talk had become general and somewhat silly. Even Mike and Erin had been given a watered-down sip of the Blue Nun wine that Aunt Lexie had brought, and though it certainly did not go with pork and sauerkraut, it seemed to mellow the old woman. Before she touched her ice cream, she stood and proposed a toast.

"To William—an honest, generous, and ardent horse."

"Hear, hear," seconded Mr. Calahan. "To a good horse. Though I don't know a thing about it."

"That you don't," his wife agreed.

Everyone touched glasses and drank to William. Tawnya Calahan proposed a second toast.

"To the bear! May he find a happy home in the state park, a home so dear that he never wants to leave it."

"To the bear," Mike echoed.

The ice cream, Erin thought longingly, was melting. Everyone touched glasses and drank to the health of the bear.

"To the old gray mare!" Don Calahan proposed, glass lifted high.

"Spindrift is not an old gray mare!" Erin protested.

"*She's* not," said Aunt Lexie primly, "but I certainly am. Swaybacked, and getting long in the tooth."

"Exactly," said Mr. Calahan. "To Aunt Lexie Bromer, who ain't what she used to be. She's not a stranger anymore."

The clink of glasses was a warm and friendly sound. Erin no longer cared about the melting ice cream. Aunt Lexie's face had changed, had softened.

"Well," she muttered, "I've heard about deaths bringing people together, but I never thought . . ."

"To the ice cream," said Mike without lifting a glass, and they all took spoons and attended to it.

Aunt Lexie stayed late, talking. She had a number of stories to tell, not all about horses, and a razor-sharp wit when she told them. On toward the end of the evening, though, without much effort, she began talking about William again.

"It was a shock," she said. "I have to admit it. I don't know when I've felt so . . . old. But, you know, thinking about it, I'm glad he went quickly. It's when they're suffering, and you have to make a decision to put them down—that's when it really breaks your heart."

"You've had horses die before?" asked Mike.

"Oh, yes. Not many, thank God. But I guess— I guess I just thought William would live forever."

Silent sympathy all around.

"Do you know what really bothers me?" Aunt Lexie asked, not expecting an answer. "Especially about William. It's having to call the rendering plant."

"Huh?" said Mike.

"They send a truck out to take the animal, and they haul it off and make it into leather and grease and dog meat and bonemeal and . . . glue, I guess." Her voice faltered for a moment, and Erin sat very still, feeling sick.

"My poor William. . . . But there's really nothing else I can do, except have a man in with a backhoe to dig a grave, and that costs."

"I always thought that stuff about the glue factory was a joke," said Mrs. Calahan, sounding dazed. "I mean, I thought that all stopped years ago. Aren't there cemeteries for horses?"

"Nothing around here. In big cities, maybe, but they cost a bundle, too. You know, people around here think I'm rich, but I'm not. It's all tied up in land and horses. You know what's buying my groceries? Your board money."

Mr. Calahan had been thinking rather than listening. When he spoke he seemed to be far off the subject. "I have to shoot a wedding Saturday," he said. "But if you can hold off till Sunday, Mike and Erin and I can dig you a hole. I don't know how long it'll take us, though."

Aunt Lexie first gaped, then looked as if she might cry. Then she made some visible changes in her thinking.

"Can't hold off till Sunday," she said briskly. "He'll start to swell and stink before then. And it's a nice thought, but there's some sort of ordinance against it, anyway, groundwater contamination or whatever. Nope, some things really just can't be helped. The Hide and Tallow people are coming tomorrow."

Erin looked at the floor. She hoped they would be gone before she got home from school.

"And, you know, William's gone. It really doesn't matter to him one way or the other," Aunt Lexie added thoughtfully. "Guess I'm just sniffling for myself. . . ." She heaved herself up off the sofa, straightening slowly. "Well, I ought to get home. Thank you all. Best dinner I've had since I don't know when. I don't generally cook much for myself."

"Come again soon," said Tawnya Calahan promptly. "Let's set a date right now."

"Cripes, I'd love to." The old bag sounded almost touched. "But I hate to—when I can't have you over—I mean, my place just isn't . . ."

Have us in the tack room, Erin thought.

"No problem. You come here. First Friday in June sound okay?"

"Okay." Aunt Lexie swallowed. "I'll bring the wine."

Erin went to bed after Aunt Lexie left, but it was a good while before she slept. She was thinking.

Spindrift was out in the paddock closest to the barn when Erin arrived at the farm the next day.

Aunt Lexie was nowhere to be seen, but Spindrift greeted Erin with a sulky look and ambled away from her, plodding with a poor-old-horse air to the paddock's farthest corner, where she stood with her tail toward her mistress. Erin smiled. She knew that the mare, though she refused to come when she was called, would stand grumpily and let herself be caught. She just had to have her say about work and humans.

"I'll fake you out today," muttered Erin.

She had something else to do besides ride. She walked slowly past Spindrift's paddock and down the lane to the paddock by the woods. The Hide and Whatever people had been there, thank God— William's body was gone. The gate still hung open, and Erin nodded at it. Aunt Lexie probably would not use this paddock for a while.

Erin went in and looked around. She got on her hands and knees, hunting. It took her a good hour to find the pipe—it had landed in the weeds beyond the fence. When at last she had it, she took it up and put it on a ledge in the stable, where the old bag would be sure to find it if she wanted it.

Chapter Eleven

"Whoa, girl, good wossie."

With sponges, towels, a garden hose, a bucket of suds, and one of bleach for the hocks and tail, Erin was giving Spindrift a bath. She had the mare tethered in the driveway outside the stable, and for the most part, Spindrift was standing quietly. Even so, Erin was struggling. Bathing a horse is at least as large a job as washing a car, and Erin had gotten nearly as wet as Spindrift. Seated on a lawn chair well out of hose range, Aunt Lexie was watching with amusement.

"Whoa, girl, good baby—" The mare shook her head again, and Erin stood back with frothy clumps of suds clinging to her T-shirt. "Why won't she let me shampoo her mane?"

"Most of them are funny about their ears and their polls. Ticklish up there. Start down lower, and work your way up."

Erin did.

"At least she didn't go bananas when you hosed her down."

"Probably felt good. I think she liked it."

"She should. It's hot enough."

The school year was over at last, just the day before. Now that Erin had more time, Mr. Calahan wanted to take some pictures of her on Spindrift. But no amount of brushing ever made the mare look clean—dirt showed on her white coat, and grass stained it. So did manure. She looked like a pinto. Like most horses of a different color, she seemed to aspire to be brown, or at least beige.

"Make sure she doesn't roll after you're done with her. Every little speck shows on that one. That's what comes of buying such a flashy critter."

Erin made a face at Aunt Lexie and set to work trying to bleach the stains out of Spindrift's tail and off her hocks.

"Who's that standing up along the road?" Aunt Lexie asked suddenly. "I've seen her up there before, from time to time."

Erin shaded her eyes to look. "It's Marcy. She's nice, Aunt Lexie. You should see the card she gave me when I was laid up."

"What sort of card?"

"A drawing of Spindrift. She really loves horses. I'm going to ask her down." Erin signaled so eagerly that she knocked herself off balance.

"You're going to spook your horse."

Spindrift stood quietly, looking scornful, as Erin, swinging her arms like a windmill, stumbled into her bucket of suds, soaking one foot. She stood red-faced as Marcy came slowly down the driveway. But Marcy seemed impressed by the chaos.

"I never knew you could bathe a horse!"

"I should have done it weeks ago, the first hot day. They get really gross over the winter." Erin dumped the remaining suds and the bucket of bleach over Spindrift. "But all I wanted to do was ride."

"I bet," Marcy mumbled, staring at the mare.

"You'll find," Aunt Lexie boomed, "that it's almost as much fun working 'em from the ground."

"Marcy, do you know Mrs. Bromer?"

Erin felt quite certain that Marcy knew who Aunt Lexie was, just as well as Aunt Lexie knew who Marcy was. But Aunt Lexie would require an introduction, just as she required her "Aunt." So Erin did her duty; Aunt Lexie heaved herself out of her lawn chair and shook Marcy's hand, and Marcy said a polite hello. She sounded scared.

"So," Aunt Lexie said with a sharp stare, "you're another one who likes my horses."

"I— They're beautiful. But I love all kinds of horses."

Erin adjusted the garden hose and went to work rinsing the soap and shampoo off Spindrift. The mare didn't like the spray near her face. Erin could not coax her to stand still while her neck and mane were being rinsed. Aunt Lexie and Marcy stood watching silently.

"Fill a bucket," Marcy suggested at last, "and use that."

"My very thought." Aunt Lexie looked at Marcy curiously. "You've been around horses?"

"No."

Silence, as Erin filled a bucket and poured it behind Spindrift's ears. The mare shook herself, showering Erin, and everyone laughed.

"But I'd love to have one," Marcy declared in a burst of confidence. "Just—any one. It wouldn't have to be a beautiful one like Spindrift. Just any horse at all. . . ." Her voice dwindled away on a note of longing that Erin recognized all too well. She stood fumbling with the bucket handle. It made her feel uncomfortable to have something that Marcy so badly wanted.

"Sweat scraper," Aunt Lexie told her crisply. "On the bench, Erin."

She picked up a towel instead. "Maybe you'll have one someday, Marcy," she said.

"Not a chance." Marcy seemed sadly certain of that. "My folks are divorced, and half the time Dad doesn't send the money. My mom's car is just about shot, and she doesn't know how she's going to get another one."

Stuck for an answer, Erin towel-dried Spindrift as best she could. The mare's mane and tail hung stringily. "Tangle remover," said Aunt Lexie, reaching up onto her porch for the pump-spray container.

"Well," said Marcy, "I have to go home."

"Already?" Erin protested. "You just got here."

"My mom'll want me home. She's always afraid my dad's going to kidnap me or something." Marcy shrugged. "Most days, after school, I'm not allowed out till she gets home from work, or I would have been here sometimes to watch you ride."

"Hi yi yi," Erin said, dazed. "What do you do in the summer when she works?"

"She's a teacher out at Vo-Tech. She doesn't work summers."

"You mean she's home now?" Aunt Lexie cut in sharply.

"Uh-huh. Hey, I've got to—"

"There's a phone in the tack room." Aunt Lexie pointed with one outstretched, leathery hand. "Go in there and call her, tell her you're here with Erin and me. Tell her you have to stay and help Erin walk that horse dry. You want me to talk to her?" Coming from Alexandra Bromer, that sounded like a threat.

"N-no. Okay, I'll try it." Marcy fled to the tack room. Aunt Lexie bent over with a grunt—her back still hurt her. Hissing between her teeth, she sprayed great bursts of tangle remover onto Spindrift's tail.

"*Cripes,*" she muttered.

Erin took the tangle remover from her and did the mane.

"It worked!" Marcy came out of the tack room with a surprised smile. "I can stay awhile."

"Good," said Aunt Lexie sharply, stomping into the tack room. Marcy gave her a sideward glance, her eyes showing a flash of white. She looked, Erin thought, like a startled filly. Then she tossed back her palomino hair and came over to stand by Spindrift's head.

"Can I—may I—touch her?"

"Sure," said Erin. "Pat her on the neck. She's funny about her nose."

"Here." Aunt Lexie came out with an extra comb. "You do the mane."

During the next hour Marcy learned the basics of leading a horse as they walked Spindrift dry. Aunt Lexie watched for a while, then went off to sit on her porch, chewing her pipe thoughtfully. After Marcy had to leave, Erin put Spindrift into a paddock and watched, resigned, as the mare rolled in the grass, putting greenish stains on herself. The photo session would not take place for a couple of weeks, anyway. This had been only a first bathing. Erin helped Aunt Lexie coax the foals in for feeding and handling. Then she went home. When she got there, on an impulse, she went to the phone to call Marcy. She had a feeling her friend would be coming to the stable again the next day, but they could talk about the foals, anyway, and Aunt Lexie. . . . But she could not find the Gilmore number in the directory. The information operator told her it was unlisted.

When she arrived at the stable the next morning, Marcy was already there, standing by the fence up along the road, watching and waiting.

"You could go on down," Erin told her. "I don't think she'd bite you."

"Who, the horse or Mrs. Bromer?" Marcy laughed nervously. "It's you I come to see, anyway."

"I know better," Erin teased.

"No, really—"

Once at the barn, Erin asked Marcy for her phone number and scrawled it on the calendar in the tack room. Then she had her friend hold Spindrift by the halter and lead chain while she brought the clippers. Spindrift's whiskers and bridle path needed to be trimmed, and because she was touchy about her whiskers she needed a lot of sweet talk and holding. Erin did her fetlocks first, until the mare became used to the sound of the clippers. Then the bridle path, the area of clipped mane behind the ears that set off her forelock. Marcy offered handfuls of hay to get Spindrift to keep her head down while Erin took care of that and the ears.

"Now the whiskers," said Erin. "With horses, you always save the worst for last." Rule eleventy-two.

Hooves clopped on the gravel outside, and Aunt Lexie came in, leading one of the broodmares.

"Does she need to be vetted?" Erin asked. The broodmares were seldom stabled unless they were foaling. They stayed in their pasture, where a run-in shelter stood along the far fence with its wind-break of poplar trees. Only colts in training were usually stabled.

"Nope." Aunt Lexie cross-tied the mare at the other end of the aisleway.

"Going out to stud?" Erin was guessing.

"Nope. Didn't send any of them out to stud this year. I told you, I'm getting out of this breeding business. You get done there, Marcy, you can help me groom her. It gets me in the back, trying to reach under the belly."

"Really?" Marcy dropped Spindrift's lead to the floor and went over to pat the other mare, plainly delighted. Erin could see that clipping was forgotten for the day. She cross-tied Spindrift, wondering what in the world Aunt Lexie was up to. There was an impish gleam in the old woman's eye.

"What's her name?" Marcy asked.

"Why, Babe, like all the rest of them." Aunt Lexie grinned, full of herself.

"Hi, Babe!"

"No, kiddo, I was just teasing." The old woman's grin softened into a smile. "Riddle Me Ree is her name, her registered name. You can call her Riddle, if you want. Or Ree. Here, take this and start at the top of her neck." She handed Marcy the body brush. "Short, firm strokes. Never use the hard brush on the face or below the hocks or knees."

Riddle Me Ree stood quietly through Marcy's awkward attempt at grooming. She was a sturdy, seal-brown Morgan horse, as brown as any horse could be, darkish mottled brown, with mane and tail exactly the same color as the rest of her, and not a white hair on her anywhere. The effect was handsome but mysterious. What on earth was Aunt Lexie up to? Erin stood doing nothing, wondering. No use asking the old bag, judging by the smirk on her face. She couldn't really mean to sell all the horses, could she? Not standing there smiling the way she was. . . .

"You going riding, Erin?" Aunt Lexie turned to her suddenly, startling her out of her trance.

"Later." Erin put the clippers away.

"Good. Bring a saddle for Riddle, would you? But let her sniff it first. She hasn't been saddled in a good ten years."

Erin went, her mind making exclamation points all the way to the tack room. Riddle blew at the saddle doubtfully, but she stood still as Erin swung it onto her back.

"Stand at her head, Marcy, and hold the halter. No, this way. . . . Now, Erin, be careful and go slowly. Fasten that girth real loose, just enough to keep the saddle on. She was a little cinchy, if I remember right."

Riddle danced about uneasily. "Whoa, Babe," Marcy told her, pronouncing it "ho," the way Erin and Aunt Lexie did. "I mean whoa, Riddle. Ho, ho, ho, ho, Ree—"

"You sound like Santa Claus," said Erin.

"She wasn't too bad at all." Aunt Lexie seemed relieved. "Now, Marcy, you just put a chain on her and undo those cross ties and lead her around until she gets used to the feel of it."

Erin could stand the wondering no longer. "Are you going to sell her?" she blurted.

"Nope." Aunt Lexie was grinning again. "Most of the others, yes, but maybe not her. Not just yet. She used to be a real mannerly riding horse."

Marcy stood with the cross ties not yet undone, as if she were frozen in place, with her lips parted just a little. The question she wanted to ask would not yet come.

Aunt Lexie waved her pipe in a large gesture.

"The way I see it, having one kid around has been so—well, interesting—" She rolled her eyes at Erin. "I might as well try it with a few more. Maybe take some boarders, let them help with the work. Maybe give some lessons. Riddle, here, might be my lesson horse."

Other boarders! New horses, people to ride with. Lessons! Maybe Marcy . . .

"We'll see. I have to try her out." Aunt Lexie leaned at her ease against a stall. "Marcy, I'll need you to help."

"Me?" Marcy sounded as if she could barely speak.

"Oh, Erin, too, of course. But Erin's too darn experienced these days. You don't know how to ride, do you?" Aunt Lexie scowled suddenly, making Marcy take a step back.

"N-no. Not at all."

"Good. You'll do. I need you to learn to ride on her. So I can see how she does."

The suspense had been drawn out for too long. At this news, both girls burst into shrieks of excited joy, forgetting the most basic rule: No noise in the stable. Luckily, Spindrift and Riddle both had sense. They stood looking blank as the girls danced about in the aisleway between them. Quite carried away, Erin darted over to Aunt Lexie, gave her a bear hug and kissed her. Marcy followed and did likewise, more slowly.

"*Good* heavens," said Aunt Lexie, far more startled than the horses. "Confound it, Erin, you've made me drop my pipe."

Chapter Twelve

It was nearly two weeks before Marcy mounted Riddle for her first lesson on horseback. Before that could happen, the mare had to get used to saddle, bridle, and rider again. Erin was given the job of working with her. Aunt Lexie coached. The process could be taken only a step or two further each day, so that Riddle would not feel abused and rebel. At first Erin only leaned her weight on the mare's back, or put one foot in the stirrup from the ground. When she finally mounted, she settled her weight in the saddle very lightly and only for a moment. Riddle was bunched to buck. But the mare quickly lost her fear and proved willing, moving almost gaily around the ring. Erin found that Riddle was more highly trained than Spindrift, far more yielding to leg. All the same, she was happy to be able to turn her attention back to her own horse.

"I'm going to try riding her bareback," she told Aunt Lexie, leaning on the rail with the old woman and watching Marcy ride Riddle around and around at the walk.

"Fine," Aunt Lexie said. "Good for your seat. Just try it in the ring first. And wear moccasins or something."

"Huh?"

"Or sneakers. Soft shoes."

"Oh." Erin glanced down at her well-worn boots. She would have to wear her running shoes tomorrow.

"Shorten up on your reins a little, Marcy!" Aunt Lexie called. "That's it! You're looking real good!"

"Hey," said Erin, amazed, "you were never that nice to me!" Then she thought. "Or—is Marcy doing better than I did?"

"No, kiddo, you always did fine." Aunt Lexie surprised her by reaching over and giving her shoulders a quick, one-armed hug. "Marcy's doing fine, too. But I think I'm learning as much as either of you."

"Huh?"

"Never mind, kid." Aunt Lexie was sucking on her pipe. "Get your feet back just a little, Marcy! Drop your heels. That's good!"

Erin ambled off to groom Spindrift and tack her up. Her father had at last found some free time in which to take his photographs, and Spindrift had been bathed yet again, put in a clean, clean stall and draped in a stable sheet in hopes that she would stay white for a few minutes, rather than putting brown spots on herself. When she saw Erin, she swung around in a bored way to put her rump toward the girl.

"Hello, Grumpo." The stall, Erin saw, was no longer very clean. "Made me some nice manure, I see. Get any on yourself?"

She opened the stall door and coaxed Spindrift over to her with a slice of apple, standing patiently while the mare turned around slowly, with distrust. It was all part of Spindrift's way. Finally Spindrift could resist the treat no longer, and one labored step at a time she came to get it, stretching her neck for it from as far away as she could manage. Erin smiled and shook her head, pulling the apple slice back a little.

"No, fuzzyface, you have to come right up to me. That's it. One more step— Oh, you did put a spot on yourself. Of course."

Twenty minutes later Erin had Spindrift ready and led her out. The mare danced about, sensing excitement. Erin's father was there, setting up one of his largest cameras on a tripod. Spindrift snorted and blew at it doubtfully, and Aunt Lexie came over to inspect the mare.

"Full of it," she said dryly.

"Always," said Mr. Calahan.

Vague smudges showed on Spindrift's white rump in the sunlight. "Cornstarch," Aunt Lexie said to Erin.

"Huh?"

"Brush some cornstarch through those. It's in the tack room." What wasn't? "Here, I'll hold her while you go get it."

Mr. Calahan stood studying the photo angles. Erin struggled with cornstarch, and by some miracle got none on herself. Ready at last, she mounted Spindrift and cantered her around the paddock a few times to settle her. Mr. Calahan had chosen a spot at the head of the lane, with the woods and pasture as a background. He waved his daughter into position. Aunt Lexie had gone back to Marcy and her lesson, and could be heard hollering.

"Head up, Marcy! Look toward where you're going. That's better."

Erin smoothed Spindrift's mane nervously with her left hand. "Her mane's on the wrong side for English," she told her father. "It's still on the western side. I never bothered training it the other way."

"Mmph," said her father, down behind his camera, focusing.

From where she sat, Erin could study Marcy, horse and all. Marcy did indeed look good on Riddle. Her mother, who seemed to be a fussy sort, had outfitted her completely in spotless buff-colored breeches, shiny-black English riding boots, a black velveteen hunt cap and a ratcatcher shirt with monogram. Erin took off her bicycling helmet for the photographer, hiding it on her far side. She looked down sadly at her jeans—her newest pair, but jeans all the same. She had polished her boots, but they still showed the scuffs and crinkles of months of wear. Brown, frontier-style boys' boots, bought at Kinney's.

"I sure don't look like much of an English rider," she said to her father.

"Mmmm," he said, fussing with his lens. Then he looked up at Erin.

"I don't think there was ever any thought of turning you into a show-style rider," he said. "Who could afford it?"

Silence, as Mr. Calahan made a final check of his equipment settings.

"You know why we got you that horse?" he asked Erin suddenly.

"Because I wanted it!"

"Nope. Smile." Click. "If parents got kids whatever they wanted, whenever they wanted, just because they wanted it—"

"Okay, okay," Erin interrupted, rolling her eyes and taking Spindrift in a circle—the mare was starting to fidget, and so was she.

"There, that's good, right there. No, we got that horse because we hoped it would be good for you."

"Huh?"

"It looked like the only thing that might bring you

out of your shell. Can't you smile?" Two more clicks.

The smile was puzzled. Erin had not known she had been in a shell.

"It took nerve for you to talk to Aunt Lexie that first time, and it took some doing for you to work things out with us, and we liked seeing that, your mother and I." Mr. Calahan took a break from the photography for a while, looking at her as he talked. "So we thought, go with it. And we're glad we did."

"You weren't at first," Erin said.

"It was rough at first, wasn't it?" Don Calahan glanced up at her, smiling. "I guess none of us realized what a big step it was. But it just took you a little while to adjust, and then you started taking on a lot more responsibility, here and at home. When you stopped expecting everything to be laid in your lap on a platter, and went out and lined up baby-sitting jobs— You know, you grew six inches, right in front of my eyes."

In a distant way Erin understood what he meant. The babysitting did cut into her riding time, especially now that summer was here. She had known that it would. She had also known it was the right thing to do.

"And I haven't noticed you holing up in your room

much lately. That alone is worth more than what we paid for Spindrift."

"Me?" Erin protested. "Hole up in my room?"

Mr. Calahan ducked behind his camera, not quite hiding his amusement. "How about if you get off her for a while, and I'll take some shots of you standing at her head."

Silence for the space of three more photos. Erin was glad Spindrift's long mane fell on her near side, after all. It was so pretty.

"But that's not all," Don Calahan went on as if there had been no pause. "I'm not sure why, but it seems to me that you've been a lot more confident since you've had that horse. You've been speaking up and standing up for yourself. Maybe it's because having the horse gives you some leverage with the other kids."

"Nuh-uh," said Erin, stroking Spindrift. If anything, it had made them dump on her, she thought. Not that it mattered.

"Because you've had to work with Aunt Lexie?"

"Not really. . . ."

"Well, let me get some close-ups." Mr. Calahan turned his attention to changing his lens.

Her father understood a lot, Erin thought in awe.

But if Mr. Calahan had ever ridden a horse he loved, he would know what it was that had changed her. That feeling of being on Spindrift's back, her partner, almost a part of the horse, power between her knees, under her control—how could she be afraid of anything anymore when she had such a powerful ally, a friend, almost? No dream horse could have done for her what Spindrift had. And Spindrift was so beautiful, so real, Spindrift, the grump. And riding her filled Erin with such a feeling of . . . peace.

No need to tell Erin to smile. She was smiling, a marvelous smile. Don Calahan took three of the most cherished close-ups of his career.

"Well, Sq— Well, Erin," he said softly, "anyway, you've done a lot of growing up in a very short time."

"You know," Erin said in a sort of wonder, "lately, I'm not even afraid of Aunt Lexie anymore."

"Aunt Lexie is another matter." Don Calahan laughed and thumped his daughter on the shoulder. Whistling under his breath, he picked up his camera, tripod and all, and went off to take some shots of the foals in the pasture.

Marcy, done with her lesson, was leading Riddle back to the barn. Aunt Lexie waved at Erin and beckoned her to come over. The old hag was eyeing her house, Erin saw. She was leaning in the stable doorway and chewing on her pipe.

"I've been thinking," Aunt Lexie said. "You know, with the good weather here, there's no reason I couldn't have you folks over for something *outside*. And Marcy and her mother, too. Some sort of barbecue or picnic. Hot dogs, hamburgers—"

"We have a big grill we could bring," said Erin promptly. "Ask my dad."

"I will. We can eat and sit around on lawn chairs and watch the horses. If I can just get the porch cleaned up some, and the kitchen. . . ."

"Marcy and I can help," Erin said. "Hey, Marcy!"

"I heard," Marcy called from the aisleway. "Sure, I'll help."

"I bet Mike would help, too," said Erin, surprised at her own idea, yet certain that he would. "I'll ask him."

"You do that. Tell him next rainy day," said Aunt Lexie. "No use wasting good weather on housecleaning." Her old eyes looked dreamy. "Potato salad," she said vaguely, " and some Japanese lanterns, maybe, for after dark. Or those candles that keep the bugs away. . . ."

Erin went for a ride.

She could never remember, after she came back to the stable, what it was that she had seen, so much, or any wonderful event that could explain her great happiness. Blue violets in the grass, new green ferns, leaves like small, soft hands brushing her face—but she could have seen all those things, walking. It was the riding itself, the process, rhythmic movement and warm sunshine, Spindrift's eager step and bobbing head and the rich horse-and-leather smell of her, the way her white ears swiveled half around when Erin spoke to her, the soft white fringe of fur on those ears. . . . Spindrift pricked her ears toward everything she scented or saw. Was it all right? Yes, Erin said it was. The gentle voice, the feel of the firm seat on her back, the knowledge that she had someone with her, Erin riding her, gave her peace and courage. A proud horse, a bold horse, she carried her head calm and high.

"Dad's proud of me," Erin told her.

A flicker of a white ear. All was well.

"You just wait till Marcy and Riddle can ride with us. We'll get you past that bad place where the bear scared you. . . . I think Marcy's a friend. She likes me."

Even tempo of hooves, muted in loam, beneath

trees. A soft snort. A birch catkin dropped on Spindrift's neck, and she shook away the itch like a dog, startling Erin into laughter.

"You've mussed your mane." Erin smoothed it down. "Pretty girl. Old gray grouchy mare. What has got into Aunt Lexie, I wonder. I think she likes me, too."

Spindrift fluttered her ears and twitched the skin of her neck—an early deer fly was bothering her. Erin reached forward and swatted it for her.

"Let's have a canter, okay?"

Did she say a canter? Hi ho, here we go. Gaily the little mare lifted into it from the walk.

Homeward bound, through the woods at the easy canter just for the fun and challenge of it, ducking branches . . . there was a sudden noisy chatter of voices, and Spindrift shied, jumping sideways.

It was Erin's school friends, four of them, running into the woods along the path, bursting into sight from behind the laurel bushes. They had not spooked the horse badly, not really. Erin's legs, long and heels down around the horse's barrel, kept her seat for her, and her hands, held low, checked Spindrift and circled her and brought her to a halt almost before she had time to think. But the mare looked awesome when she was spooked, Erin knew. There before her stood her friends, stone-still and very silent and staring, Mikkie Orris among them.

"Hi," said Erin.

Not answering, they edged toward the side of the path. Spindrift was still snorting and rolling her eyes at them.

"It's okay," Erin told them. "Really." It had been a while, she realized suddenly, since any of them had called her Dipstick. And they didn't look as if they were about to now.

"Hey, Erin," said Mikkie, her eyes on the horse, "you think Old Lady Bromer would give me riding lessons?"

"Ask her," Erin said. "But call her Mrs. Bromer. Well, see ya."

"See ya," they all echoed, voices muted, and Erin rode on, thoughtful. She had seen a familiar longing on the face of the red-haired girl.

"Let's not go home just yet, Spindrift," she said suddenly, and she turned the mare in a new direction, riding her along the fringes of Terrace Heights.

It took a while until she found a way to get through to her house. She did not want to offend any neighbors by leaving hoofprints on their lawns. Sticking to the weedy stretches and vacant lots, she had to watch for remnants of old barbed-wire fences. But in due time, with patience, she rode Spindrift along the quiet end of her street and into her own driveway. Her mother, planting marigolds, turned toward the clop of hooves and stood up, brows arched in surprise.

"Hi, Mom," Erin greeted her. "Spindrift wants to give you a big, green, sloppy kiss."

"No, thank you!" But Tawnya Calahan came over and patted the horse's neck. Spindrift swung her head toward her in a relaxed way.

"See? She knows you're a great mom." There, it was said, and Erin waved one hand and fled, trotting Spindrift back toward the stable.

It was almost dusk when they got there, and very quiet in the sleepy bird-singing way of summer evenings. No one was around. Aunt Lexie had gone into her house for supper. Erin cooled Spindrift, grooming her for a long time. "*Good* wossie," she told the mare, hugging her around the neck, and for once Spindrift did not turn away from the caress, but grumpily bore it. Erin scratched Spindrift on her favorite place, the crest just above the withers, the place where horses like to rub one another. Then she put her into her stall to await her evening oats.

"Not my turn to feed. But dinner will be coming any minute."

Looking sulky, Spindrift turned her back, and Erin laughed softly, warm with affection.

"All right, Spunko, be that way." There, the mare had her barn name at last. "You're a super horse. I love you just the way you are."

Spindrift swung her head around to eye her, looking very white in the dusky light. Erin grinned at the mare, then lazily turned her own back, leaning against the stall and yawning. Time to go home—but it had been such a fantastic day, she hated to have it end. . . .

A soft snort sounded near her ear, and then a familiar nose, a large, dark, rubbery nose, poked through the stall bars. Familiar, but never so friendly before—the mare was nibbling at her hair! Astonished, Erin spun around.

"You couldn't possibly be that hungry!" she exclaimed.

Spindrift's nose came yet closer, only an inch from her own—and with a powerful noise the mare blew straight into Erin's nostrils.